REBEL YULE

A ROOKIE REBELS NOVEL

KATE MEADER

This novel is a work of fiction. Any references to historical events, real people, or real places are used fictitiously. Other names, characters, places, and events are products of the author's imagination, and any resemblance to actual events or places or persons, living or dead, is entirely coincidental.

Copyright © 2021 by Kate Meader

Cover design by Qamber Designs

Editing: Kristi Yanta

Copyediting: Kimberly Cannon

Proofreading: Julia Griffis, The Romance Bibliophile

ISBN: 978-1-954107-07-6

All rights reserved.

No part of this book may be reproduced in any form or by any electronic or mechanical means, including information storage and retrieval systems, without written permission from the author, except for the use of brief quotations in a book review.

1

Erik Jorgenson had fallen ass over skates for a woman twice in his life.

The first time ... well, the less said about that the better. He had screwed up and it haunted him to this day.

The second time was different. At least when it happened before, he suspected the object of his affection felt *some* smattering of affection toward him. This time, he was certain that the woman sitting behind the desk outside the office of Chicago Rebels CEO Harper Chase hated his guts.

What he didn't know was why.

Casey Higgins, assistant to Harper, didn't seem like the kind of woman who would hold a grudge. If anything, she got along perfectly fine with everyone, doling out cheery greetings and wide smiles like candy. Sugar sweet, bad-for-your-diet candy, or in this case bad for Erik's ego because none were for him. Her smile was the first thing he'd noticed when he came into the office for an appointment with Harper a year ago.

Erik had been struck.

Not because she had gorgeous legs that tapered to perfect ankles and sexy heels.

Not because she had lush waves of dark hair—really big fucking hair, if he was being honest—that he now regularly imagined gripping in his fingers.

Not even because she had eyes the color of a Swedish summer sky that lit up the room and made his pulse go boom-boom-boom like it was headed to the blue zone.

All those things were amazing, but it was the smile that clobbered him like a puck to the balls.

Back when he met her that first time, Devin in Accounting had been showing her the photocopier. She'd pressed a button, maybe the wrong button? Whatever happened, it was considered funny by the people who considered such things funny, and she smiled. A big, sunshine, all-are-welcome-here grin that made Erik think: that woman is worth knowing.

She had turned then, the smile still on her lips, and locked eyes with Erik who was standing there like an idiot waiting to be noticed. Her grin stumbled slightly, crumbled around the edges. That was okay. People were sometimes nervous around the players, not that he was a superstar or anything. He had been on the team for the last seven years, as first goaltender for five, and rarely earned the mob-like attention showered on his teammates. But people were often apprehensive at meeting pro-athletes.

"Hi," he had said. Very profound. "I'm Erik. Pleasure to meet you." He had extended his hand and she had looked at it like it was a gun or a bomb.

There was an awkward pause that stretched to down-right uncomfortable. Accounting Guy Devin had to jump in, that's how weird it was.

"This is Casey Higgins. She's Harper's new PA," he said.

"Started yesterday but she's already broken the photocopier." He laughed, confirming ha-ha-not-really-broken-just-funny and Erik assumed it was amusing, or had been about sixty seconds ago.

Not anymore.

Casey's smile had vanished, her sun ducking behind a raincloud. Not a natural fade away, this was abrupt. She met Erik's gaze and hello, total eclipse, all the light and heat drained from the room because of him.

Erik hated that. Hated that anyone would lose their joy just by looking at him.

At first he'd assumed she'd seen something behind him. On the wall was a picture of the Chicago Rebels holding the Stanley Cup, the year they won. Five years, now. That couldn't possibly be the reason for the veil of doom that had descended on the office.

(Though it was very sad that the team hadn't been in the running since.)

"Everything okay, Casey?"

She blinked, bringing herself back from someplace else, a location that wasn't all that pleasant to visit. Now she was here in *this* place with Erik, and judging by her expression the view had not improved.

"Fine, thank you." Very prim and proper. Super sexy but for the *I hate your guts* vibe threaded through it. "Mr. Jorgenson, you're on Ms. Chase's schedule but you're five minutes early."

Mr. Jorgenson? "I'm never late. It's a bad habit."

"Please take a seat. I'll see if Ms. Chase is available."

So he had, and Harper was, and when he came out of the office, Casey was nowhere to be seen.

Since that day, he had run into her several times and no matter how much he tried, the chill remained.

Any plans for the weekend, Casey?
Just relaxing.
Did you catch the game last night, Casey?
I did. You all played very well.
Want to let me take you over that desk, Casey?
Maybe another time.

So that last one was in his imagination. Polite professionalism was her superpower with an undercurrent of wouldn't-piss-on-you-if-you-were-on-fire. He might harbor a harmless, abstract fantasy or two about her hullaballoo hair, sexy heels, and—he quickly learned—excellent rack, but she had obviously made up her mind definitively about him.

Brainless jock, perhaps, or weird foreigner. For someone who worked at a professional sports organization, she really ought to be nicer to the assets.

He had tried testing the limits, seeing if he could push her to reveal how they had come to this impasse. He'd complimented her blouse, mentioned the unseasonably warm temperatures for February/October/December, lamented the banality of plane travel. Nothing cracked her shell.

Once he'd asked if she would help him pick out some clothes.

I'm PA to the CEO, Mr. Jorgenson, not your personal assistant.

Worth a shot, he'd thought.

Then a couple of nights ago, something weird happened, or weirder than usual. Today, he planned to get to the bottom of her dislike of him.

He had arrived ten minutes early for his usual monthly check-in with Harper. He could tell this really bothered Casey.

Ms. Chase is with another appointment. Perhaps you should come back in a few minutes.

Oh, I don't mind waiting.

That was what he was doing. Biding his time, sitting across from her, waiting for her to finish her phone conversation. Three weeks before Christmas, and the office was festively dressed with tinsel, sprigs of holly, and Balsam garlands, real ones that scented the office. On Casey's desk sat a Dwight Schrute bobblehead figure with what looked like—was that a Belsnickel hat? It was a tiny fur cap with little bells and leaves sewn onto it. Erik loved *The Office*, and Dwight as Belsnickel was a favorite.

Alongside the Dwight figure was a small poinsettia, its pot covered with a shiny red wrapper. Had she brought that in herself or had someone given it to her? A boyfriend, perhaps?

Jealousy dug sharp fangs into his chest, which made no sense. She wasn't interested and no matter how much he tried to make nice, it came off as unwelcome. Yet he felt in his bones that he was missing some piece of a tricky puzzle. That in another lifetime, they could mean something to each other.

Which was ludicrous.

She placed the phone down and turned back to her computer, but not before she flicked a glance his direction, one that managed to convey death and disdain.

Here we go. "Did you have fun at the Empty Net the other night?"

She raised her gaze, wrinkled her nose. Ultra cute. "Were you speaking to me?"

"Don't see anyone else here."

Lip curl of disgust. He wasn't usually a smart-ass but this woman made him want to rattle her cage.

"I had a good time."

"Really? You left pretty quickly. Theo was worried he might have offended you."

Another sharp look. Two nights ago, he and Rebels defenseman Theo Kershaw had walked into their local bar, the Empty Net, and spotted Mia Wallace, sister of their captain with a few of her pals. One of them was Tara who used to date Cal Foreman (before Mia slid into her place, kind of complicated), the other was Kennedy who was currently rooming with Reid Durand and looking after his dog (and man, that defined complicated).

Casey was also there, but not for long.

The moment Erik and Theo showed their faces, she stood and announced her departure before hightailing her hot ass out of there like her yoga pants were on fire.

Yeah, he'd noticed. (The quick departure and the sweet ass.)

"I had to get home," she said quietly. "I'd been out for a while and my ... cat needed to be fed."

As stories went, that was kind of weak. "So I can tell Theo it wasn't personal."

"I've no problem with Theo."

"Just me, then."

She skewered him with those clear blue eyes, now frozen in contempt. "I don't have a problem with anyone."

"Yet you're happy to gift smiles to everyone but me."

"I don't owe you any of my joy."

He flinched at her words, delivered with such arrowed precision.

"You're right, you don't. I apologize."

Surprise graced her pretty features before the mask of professionalism resumed. "No apology necessary."

He stood and approached the desk. Where he was

sitting was too distant for the intimate conversation this situation needed.

He touched the cap on the Dwight bobblehead. "Did you make this?"

A blush suffused her cheeks. "Yes, it's just a joke. Well, for my own amusement."

She didn't look amused. She looked uncomfortable. "You must really like the show." He'd been a fan himself ever since the night he ... best not to dwell on that. On the heartache of his own making.

Casey moved the Dwight bobblehead a half-inch to the right and went back to her computer screen.

"Casey, you started working here about a year ago, I believe."

"Hmm, hmm." Tip-tap on her keyboard, no eye contact, wave lines of derision.

"And I've come in here for several appointments and each time, you've been sort of ... cool toward me. Unusually so."

She peered up at him through the veil of her dark lashes. Some odd range of emotion cycled through, sadness to anger to the smooth expression firmly back in place. It took all of one point five seconds.

"I'm sorry if you think I've been unprofessional."

"No, you've been very professional. But I get the impression—more than an impression—that I've done something to offend you. I wish I knew what it was."

Her lips twitched. She clearly had something to say, an explanation that would blow this tension between them wide open. Five seconds passed. Ten. Fifteen.

"You've done nothing. Absolutely nothing."

A shiver corkscrewed down his spine, like the premonition he sometimes got before a game when the pipes were as wide as a football field and he was as small as a gnat trying to fight off the puck.

Why did he feel like absolutely nothing meant exactly that? He was supposed to have done *something*, and his *not* doing it had screwed things up.

"Casey—"

The door to Harper's office opened and the boss's ten o'clock walked out.

"Ms. Chase is ready to see you now," Casey said.

She turned back to her computer, dismissing him with more than words.

CASEY HIGGINS WAS LIVING the dream.

A job she loved, working for a great boss and an organization that treated its employees as well as the pro-athletes they served.

A cute apartment with a reasonable rent and a landlord who fixed things when she needed (and didn't leer at her like the last one did).

A grumpy kitty-cat she adored, and while he didn't adore her back, she knew—just knew—he felt about as much affection as his species would allow.

She was an independent woman, who had thrown off the shackles of servitude to—scratch that.

She was doing just fine on her own, *thankyouverymuch*. And if sometimes she clutched her cat a little too closely or drank that third glass of wine while binge-watching *Bridgerton* for the fifth time or got a touch misty-eyed when her boss's husband sent her flowers just because—well, that was normal, wasn't it? Merely a smidge of melancholy because everyone longed for someone to lean on.

Then she would snap right out of it and affirm the mantra she'd been using to boost herself for the last year.

You don't need a special someone to feel special. You don't need anyone at all.

Except sometimes the positive talk lowered in volume around the holidays.

Sometimes it diminished to barely a whisper at a holiday party, or just prior to one. When you had to get ready, look yourself in the mirror, and assure your lazy-ass brain that once you arrived at said party, you'd have a rollicking good time.

"Casey, why are you still here?" Harper Chase, the Chicago Rebels CEO and amazing boss lady, click-clacked out of her office and stopped at Casey's desk. "Everyone's leaving early to get their glad rags on for the party."

Casey checked the time on her computer screen. Only 4:10pm. "I brought my dress and was going to change here. I just have a few things to finish up."

Harper frowned, activating a divot between her eyebrows. More of a dimple, really. Anyone else seeing that expression might be concerned that the petite blonde with the ball-busting attitude was about to go off on them. But Casey had worked in the Rebels' front office for just over a year and she knew Harper's moods and tics. This was concerned Mama Bear.

"You work too hard. I try to be a good boss and shoo you out of here early on Fridays, but does it do any good?"

"It's just a couple of things. I was working on the stats report for the trade discussion meeting on the day we return." Casey enjoyed compiling reports and Harper loved reading them: they were both analysts to the bone. Harper sometimes even asked her opinion. "And Holly in PR called about setting up a meeting with Dex O'Malley."

Harper sighed. "I hate being such a killjoy before the holidays but that boy needs to be taken in hand."

Dex was a newly-acquired forward who, since arriving from Nashville a month ago, had jumped into Chicago nightlife with the enthusiasm of a child in a Chuck E. Cheese ball pit.

An E. coli-infected one.

Often photographed in the company of multiple models (usually at the same time) he hadn't done anything outrageous or damaging to the org yet. But Harper wanted to nip it in the bud before his life—and the team—became fodder for the gossip rags.

"Like I don't have enough on my plate with Durand losing his shit the other night." Reid Durand had knocked out his brother Bastian, a player on the Hawks during the crosstown classic game a few days ago. Durand Jr. was okay but it resulted in an ejection and a one-game suspension for Reid, just when he had started to play to his full potential at center.

"I think he might have some things on his mind."

"Yeah, I heard. The dog nanny drama." Harper shook her head. "Maybe Remy could chat with him tonight. He's good at the heart-to-heart business. Takes his elder statesman role very seriously."

"Dex, too?"

"Hale can talk to him. It's his job after all." Hale Fitzpatrick, the new general manager, would be officially starting January 1. "I love these boys but sometimes the mothering aspect can be a bit much."

"Yet you do it so well." Casey grinned. "Speaking of, you should scoot because I'm sure you have stuff to manage for the party."

"That's why having a kept man is so useful. Remy's on

site and if anyone knows how to throw a party, it's him. But I do need to make sure the girls haven't dirtied their dresses. Knowing my pushover husband, he gave in and let them get gussied up hours ago." She smiled, seemed to hesitate, then ventured, "Bringing a date tonight?"

"To the party? Oh, God, no!" The notion shouldn't be ridiculous. Casey was twenty-nine years old, reasonably well-adjusted, and not completely hideous. There was no good reason why she shouldn't be dating except for the obvious.

Her prick of an ex had left her hollowed out.

"If you ever want me to help set you up ..." Harper let that hang before adding the kicker, "I'm pretty good at matchmaking."

"Funny because Dante insists you're terrible at it." Dante Moretti was the former general manager, now married to Cade Burnett, a Rebels D-man. "Said that he'd barely been here a month and you were trying to set him up with people who would never work."

"While he was seeing one of my players under the radar. Sometimes we only know what the heart wants when faced with what it most certainly does not. That ingrate still refuses to admit how much I helped!" She checked her watch, set in a gorgeous bracelet given to her by Remy. "Okay, I'd better head out. People will be arriving at six but stop by early so we can have a cocktail before it gets crazy."

That was so sweet of her to include Casey. "Will do."

Harper swished out, leaving the scent of jasmine in her wake and Casey alone in the empty suite. With only two days to Christmas, everyone else had left early, taking advantage of the boss's generosity to run errands and buy gifts and prepare for the party.

Casey's parents would be on a Caribbean cruise over the

holiday, something they did every year since they retired to Florida. (Because they didn't get enough sun all year round.) They had invited Casey but she usually felt like a third wheel around them, so she'd declined. She would take a couple of days in January and visit them then.

Which meant she would be alone again this Christmas. Naturally.

Agh! Don't be such a Debbie Downer.

Dream job, great apartment, grumpy cat.

An hour and sixteen minutes later, her tasks completed, she headed to the restroom to get ready. She wouldn't usually spend so extravagantly but this dress had called to her from the rack at Macy's. A dusty rose, it hugged her hips and accentuated every curve. The neckline dipped a little more than she was used to, but hey, she had cleavage she never showed at work. Or ever. Time to give the girls some air.

The privilege of showcasing abundant cleavage had cost two weeks' salary but she had wanted to treat herself. With her dark, usually unmanageable curly hair up off her neck, she looked unusually glamorous, almost good enough to be on the arm of an associate at Willebrand, Nagle, and Jones LLP.

But not quite. Andrew had worried that their relationship—an up and coming law associate and the woman who worked as paralegal to one of the senior partners—wouldn't have quite enough cachet to push him to the top. Casey had supported him, emotionally and financially through law school, talked him up to Mr. Willebrand when Andrew came in to interview, and remained resolutely two steps behind so it was clear who was boss in the relationship at the office.

What a dummy she had been.

She had one reason to be grateful. Andrew had encouraged her to seek alternative employment because he thought both of them working at the same law firm "might not look so good." So she had left a job she enjoyed and taken the position of Harper's assistant, only to find out a few weeks later that Andrew had been preparing to cut her out of his life in all areas. He'd wanted to ensure no "awkwardness" at work before he brought down the hammer of splitsville just over a year ago.

Eight years together, off and on, and now she was alone —and trying to convince herself she wasn't lonely.

She had done a good job of blocking out the negative. So she might have checked Andrew's social media every now and then. They were still friends on BookFace (shout out to Jim Halpert in *The Office*!), all part of her efforts to maintain a mature attitude to their uncoupling. *Sure, we're all adults here*, she'd said over a year ago when he told her their relationship had run its course. Like this was a natural and logical end. Like she hadn't poured everything she had into it only to be told she no longer fit with his plans for Chicago legal community domination.

Last night had been the law firm holiday party, and one of her old colleagues had shot her a text saying she missed seeing her there. All day, she had sat on her hands, avoiding the temptation to check out pictures from the gathering. It would be the usual glad-handing, photos of dear old Mr. Willebrand looking a little squirrel-eyed after one too many White Russians, and Andrew with first year associate Melanie. Fresh out of law school, fresh on the ladder. Just fresh.

Casey didn't need the reminder of how she had been so easily discarded and replaced.

She smoothed her lip gloss, and if her finger shook

while she did it, she ignored it. Tonight she would have a nice time at the holiday party and enjoy the eve of a few days off.

A final check in the mirror and she was ready to go. She stepped out of the bathroom and ran right into the one person she did not want to see.

Erik Jorgenson.

Worse, Erik Jorgenson in a hot-damn suit.

All the guys looked great on travel days, but there was something about the way the Rebels goalie looked in Hugo Boss that got her engine running.

Overheating.

Kaput.

Right now, he stood tall and oak-solid in front of the elevator bank, defending it like it was the Rebels' goal, scrolling through his phone. He had yet to see her. Maybe if she backed up a step, she could hide in the restroom until—

"Casey."

Damn! Why did her pulse give that traitorous little whoop of recognition when he said her name? At this point her mind and body should be on the same page. Lord knew she had discussed her problems enough with only her hormones and her cat to hear her.

"Oh, hi." She took a step forward, trying gamely not to let any of her senses absorb the vision that was Erik. The blond hair, freshly washed and kissing his broad suited shoulders. The trim beard that shaped his jaw like a layer of angel dust. Those sumptuously blue eyes now staring at her with terrifying intent.

Her senses were having a hard time ignoring the obvious: Erik Jorgenson was a stone-cold hottie. But her brain had yet to raise the white flag. "What are you doing here?"

"I came to take you to the party."

"What? I didn't ask you to do that." Had some part of her subconscious reached out and wished him here?

"Harper told me you needed a ride. I was over at the gym, so I figured I'd stop in and see if you were still here."

Dante was right. The woman sucked at matchmaking.

I get the impression I've done something to offend you. I wish I knew what it was.

Huh, I bet you do. Try taking another puck to the head, Mr. Goalkeeper, and see if that jogs your memory.

Erik Jorgenson would be the last man on earth she would choose to voluntarily spend a moment with.

That wasn't always the case. There was a time she would've been thrilled to have this man pick her up from work for a date. Open a door for her, pull out a chair, smile over candlelight.

But he had finished with her before they had a chance to even start.

And the worst of it was that she was left with the crushed dreams ... while he didn't remember a single thing.

2

CASEY WAS CLEARLY NOT ENJOYING this turn of events.

Erik didn't want to make her uncomfortable but when Harper called and asked if he'd give her assistant a ride to the party, he'd jumped at the chance.

It wasn't the first time the Rebels CEO had mentioned Casey. More than once, she had asked him if there was something going on—something that needed to be resolved—and he had been honest.

She doesn't like me. I don't know why but she seems to actively hate me.

Now Harper was stepping in to arbitrate. Erik had known the boss a long time and she usually had good instincts. If she thought Erik should be escorting Casey to the party, she was probably right. A fifteen-minute drive to Chase Manor might give him a clue.

But the look on Casey's face right now—hell, Erik didn't want to make her uneasy.

Yet he couldn't stop staring because she was fucking gorgeous.

"If you'd prefer to make your own way there—"

She held up a hand. "No, it's fine. You went to all this trouble. I just need to get my coat."

It was no trouble at all, but he merely nodded and waited for her return.

Maybe he should put her in a cab. For the first time he considered that he might not want to know what he did to wound her. Because that's what it felt like. Not just an offhand comment or a bad joke. Whatever he had done was felt personally in her soul.

She came out of the front office, draped in a long black coat that gave flashes of that gorgeous dress she wore beneath. Her dark hair was piled on top of her head, hints of red highlights glinting under the office lights. She wore more makeup than he'd ever seen on her. Not caked on, just different. She always looked beautiful and now she looked like a shiny Christmas bauble.

Avoiding direct eye contact, she stabbed at the elevator call button.

Yeah, definitely a cab.

He took out his phone and checked Uber. There was a driver within three minutes. On the elevator's arrival, he waited for her to step in, then followed, careful to maintain a respectful distance.

Still, he couldn't help running off his mouth. "You look great. I like your hair ... like that."

She snapped her gaze to his. Surely that couldn't offend but this was his life now, it seemed.

Something flickered in her expression, almost an easing of the tension. "Thanks," and then after a beat, "You look well, too."

"Thanks."

She turned to her phone, the tension back to thick and heavy.

He had to know. Even if it made her mad, he had to know.

"Casey, I—"

The elevator ground to a screeching halt with a noise that sounded ... not good. The way it stopped was more of a lurch, to be honest.

Casey moved toward the doors, though they were still closed. "That's weird. I don't think we're on the first floor yet."

"We're not." He pressed the door open button on the panel. Nothing. He tried the first-floor button again, which was still lit, but no joy.

There was nothing for it but to push the "call" button. "Hello, is anyone there?"

Silence.

"Hello—"

A static crackle cut him off followed by a voice that sounded both loud and tinny in the small space. "This is Sean in Security. We realize the elevator is stalled. Maintenance is on the way. Don't panic."

Don't panic. That was the advice?

Erik pressed the button again. "No one's panicking. There are two of us here, Erik Jorgenson and Casey Higgins, but we're fine." He slid a glance toward Casey. "We're fine, right?"

She stepped in close, giving him a whiff of a floral scent that curled inside his chest and took residence. "How long will it be?" she asked.

"Shouldn't be more than a few minutes," Sean said. "Hold tight."

"Will do," Erik said, then to Casey, "I'm sure they're working as fast as they can."

"Freakin' Harper," she muttered.

"Harper?"

She lanced him with a look. "Never mind."

"Well, it looks like we have some time."

"For what?"

"A chat." He leaned against the elevator wall, his hands gripping the rail behind him. "I think it's time you told me exactly what I've done to piss you off."

"We've already had this conversation. Nothing."

"Now we both know that's not true. I've worked here for seven years and I don't think it's an exaggeration to say I'm pretty well-liked."

Her expression was contempt, her words even more so. "Good for you."

"But you took an instant hate to me the first time we met. I want to know why."

She pressed the call button. "Any updates? It's getting hot in here."

Yeah, it was. Sweat should not be attractive, but a light sheen covered her forehead and a strand of hair had escaped the prison of her hairstyle, a damp curl he wanted to wrap around his little finger.

"We're going as fast as we can. Do you need medical attention?"

"No—but I"—she darted another look his way, more of annoyance than fear—"we have to be somewhere."

"Just hold tight, Miss Higgins."

Taking a few steps back, she rubbed a hand over the back of her neck.

"Are you okay?"

"I don't like enclosed spaces. I'm not full-on claustrophobic, but I don't enjoy this."

"I'll give you all the space you want. The physical space."

She didn't like that.

"Yep, that means that you're not off the hook for that question. Why do you have an absolute hate-on around me?"

"Hate-on?" She blushed and he got it. Maybe. She ... *liked* him?

"Casey, is there something you need to tell me?" He took a step closer. "About how you feel?"

"How I feel? Oh, Jorgenson, you have no idea how I feel."

Jorgenson? It sounded far too familiar. Yet they had barely exchanged a word that wasn't strained or snarky. His name on her lips like that sent a shiver through him.

He quickly revised his previous opinion. That didn't sound like unrequited love or lust.

"It's nothing. Could we stop talking about it?" She leaned over and pressed the button again, just as the elevator dipped. She wobbled on her heels ... right into his arms.

He couldn't have scripted it better.

Her hands splayed on his chest. "Oh God oh God, we're going to die."

"We're not—"

Another shift. Even Erik was worried about that one but he couldn't let on. He gripped her arms under her elbows and held her still.

"Look at me, Casey."

She shook her head, kept her gaze at throat-level so he was stuck with the top of her head. *Those red highlights ... kind of like ...*

"Casey, we're not going to die. This is just the car settling after sitting for so long."

Her eyes peeked up, gorgeous blue ones that made his pulse jump. "Really?"

"Yeah, I was an engineering geek when I was a kid.

These cars are really safe." He had no idea, of course, but this was what she needed to hear. He rubbed her arm, soothing, feeling her relax. This close, he had the oddest feeling of déjà vu.

Soft blue eyes, pleading, begging, loving ...

"Casey ..."

She was closer now, secure in his grip, her breaths shallow pants against his lips. Close enough to kiss, to release the pressure valve of all this tension, but he wanted something more—her respect.

Which meant he needed the truth.

"Tell me what I did."

Her eyes darkened to a midnight-navy. For a moment, she had forgotten that she hated him. She was welcome to return to that hate-space but not before they cleared the air.

"It doesn't ma—"

He pulled her in, his lips almost brushing hers. "Yes, it does. Just tell me. What the hell did I do to you?"

"Nothing. Maybe don't assume the world revolves around you just because you're a famous athlete."

"I don't think that." He really didn't. Ask any of the guys, and they'd confirm that he didn't really rate with women, with fans, with anyone. Sure, people liked him well enough, but he hadn't made an impact the way some of his teammates had.

He hadn't found a mate like them either.

In Sweden they had a saying: *Avund hindrar sin Herre mest*, which meant "envy is its own torturer."

Consider him tortured. He wanted what his friends had. He'd thought he had it once, but it slipped from his grasp. Now with Casey, he felt this irresistible pull toward her, which was absurd considering her obvious disdain. Why was he drawn to women he couldn't have?

"But I recognize when someone doesn't like me," he murmured.

"I'd rather not talk about it."

So there was something. "Not good enough. You've been giving me the evil eye since the first day we met—"

"Not the first day," she muttered. They were still standing inches from each other and he could feel the stirrings of an erection. Just the mere proximity to her got him as hard as the look in her eyes.

"Yes, the first day. I walked into the front office and I introduced myself and ..." at least that's how he remembered it. "And you acted like I'd killed your dog."

"Well, Erik Jorgenson, that's where your amazing memory has failed you. Because that wasn't the first day."

"Wasn't the first day what?"

"It wasn't the first day we met!"

Shock electrified his muscles and loosened his grip on her arms. They'd met before? No, he would have remembered. He would never have forgotten a woman like this. Unless ...

Shit, shit, shit. He had figured out ways to get around this, so he wasn't caught out.

"I don't—I had never met you before that day."

"Wrong. We met seven years ago and it was obviously so unremarkable that you blocked it from your mind. Now where the hell is maintenance?"

Seven years ago? He would have just started on the team, newly drafted in after playing his previous season with the Swedish Hockey League. It was a lonely time for him, away from home, not knowing anyone, trying to make his mark. But the Rebels accepted him into their hearts and showed him the ropes.

Ropes that often involved nights out on the town putting

away the booze as only the young and clueless could. At the time, he was under the legal drinking age in the US, but fame had its perks and he was never denied entry to a bar as long as he was with his Rebel teammates.

"Was I drunk?"

"Oh, you'd had a few. Not enough to give you whiskey dick, though. Everything was in working order there." She sounded so bitter.

"You mean we ..." *No* ... "We had ... sex?"

"Ding ding ding, Mr. Goaltender. That's right, we did. You fucked me and forgot and that's all there is to it."

Stunned didn't begin to describe it. Erik didn't have a lot of luck with women. Usually the ones he liked were taken and he wasn't a fan of the puck bunny in a bar scene. But seven years ago ... he'd been twenty, stupid, new to Chicago, new to everything. There were nights with the boys when he drank a lot and hooked up and probably acted like an idiot. It was a brief period when he went a little crazy with the novelty of it all.

Was Casey one of those nights? He had no reason to doubt her. And he could see why she would be hurt he didn't remember.

"So still no magical jog of the old brain cells?" She waved in front of his face. "Not coming back to you? And do *not* pretend you remember."

Seven years ago, he had met *her*. Not Casey, but the woman he had fallen hard for only to have her vanish like a Cinderella who didn't even have the decency to leave behind a shoe to clue him in.

Wait one hot second.

A number, a napkin, a night he had stored away as a painful memory followed by an arena full of regret. But that hadn't been Casey ... that was ... *fuck.*

"Casey, I—" The elevator jerked again, only this time it was into action, descending at an even, unhurried pace. But not unhurried enough. She took a step back, just as the car stopped and the doors opened.

Two maintenance guys stood in the lobby, one of the security people behind them.

"You okay, miss?"

Casey blew out a breath. "Yes! Fine. Just glad to be out of there."

Erik followed her, grateful to be on solid ground, at least physically. Mentally, he was sinking in quicksand. "Casey, can we talk?"

"No," she said without a backward glance, and walked right out the front door.

3

Seven years ago ...

This was absolutely crazy.

Casey was not the kind of girl who made out with strange men in the back of a cab, but here she was ... making out with a strange man in the back of a cab. A gorgeous strange man, only he wasn't a complete stranger. He was sort of famous, actually.

Did the gorgeous and famous cancel out the crazy? She was going with yes. Because any other conclusion would have her second-guessing her reason for coming out tonight, her reason for drinking one too many Sea Breezes, her reason for throwing caution to the wind and letting this hot hunk of man help her forget that she had been dumped two nights ago by the guy she'd thought was the one.

"He can't take his eyes off you," Amee had said about ten minutes after they walked into the Empty Net—Amee to score, Casey to drown her sorrows in vodka and cranberry juice.

Casey wasn't buying it. Sure, she had made the effort,

even went to the salon to get an auburn rinse in her hair and her usually unruly curls blown straight. She wanted to be someone different. Someone who could attract the attention of any guy here.

But even when you say that's your intention, you don't expect it to work. Deep in your heart, you know that new hair, a short skirt, and a fuck-you 'tude do not a pick-up success make. You were not suddenly worthy because if you were, you wouldn't have been dumped in the first place.

This bar was known as a Rebels player hangout, or so she'd been told. Casey loved hockey, was a huge fan of the Rebels, but she would never go to their local bar. It smacked of too much star-fuckery for her liking. She wouldn't want to look like some drooling fangirl and besides, she had a boyfriend. A third year law student who was going places.

But Andrew had said that after a year together, maybe they should take a break. The day after she graduated from Northwestern with a degree in English and Communications—and no immediate post-graduation plans or interviews—her boyfriend had said they might be too different. All because she said she didn't want to go to law school.

What he didn't like was that she scored higher on the LSATs and still turned down a spot at Northwestern Law.

Now she was single and ready to mingle, as the kids said. Twenty-one, and she felt old.

She had already downed one Sea Breeze and was trying to get the attention of the bartender for another when Amee elbowed her with far more force than necessary.

"I think that's Erik Jorgenson."

"Nah. They must have all left town by now."

The season was over and the Rebels had failed to make the playoffs. Again. None of the players should be here tonight.

"No, it is. He's with Cade Burnett—God, that Texan is so freakin' cute!"

Casey looked over, and sure enough, it was them. Cade Burnett looked like he was in the middle of a story, but every now and then his teammate's attention would wander ... to Casey. He smiled at her with this awfully droll look that said "save me from this guy" and she couldn't help laughing.

As a fan of the team she knew plenty about him. At twenty years old, Erik was a native of Örnsköldsvik in Sweden, the town that had produced more Swedish NIIL stars than any other. He was a good goalie with the potential to be great, if he received the right encouragement and coaching. She wasn't sure that would be with a team like the Rebels, which seemed to be stuck in neutral lately.

The next ten minutes was more of the same. Amee drooling, Cade talking, Erik sneaking glances her way, and Casey trying to act like a Swedish hockey superstar in her orbit was perfectly normal.

Finally he came over.

"Hi, I'm Erik and I'm in need of rescue."

"Oh, really?" *Play it cool, play it cool.* She glanced over his shoulder. Cade was staring at Erik and shaking his head, like he couldn't believe his teammate just upped and walked away mid-sentence. "Looked like a good story."

"It wasn't. Something about American football and a kicker with a lead foot. Alamo thinks he is so entertaining."

Amee grinned. "But he's so cute. And now he's so lonely."

Erik smiled at Casey, a touch of diffidence to it that made her heart flip. "Perhaps we should swap."

Casey stood and smoothed out her skirt. She might have done it on purpose to draw the attention of a hockey hunk to her legs, which were having a good day. "Sure, I'd love to hear about the kicker with the lead foot."

She made to walk away, only to have Erik place a hand on her arm. The tingles!

"Ah, funny girl."

She stopped and they stared, the moment seeming to stretch to infinity. Amee must have said something, maybe about going to talk to Cade Burnett, because the next thing Casey knew, she and Erik were alone and the Sea Breezes were flowing.

Which is why she was making out with a gorgeous strange man in the back of that cab. Only it didn't end there …

4

"Jorgenson, you're late!"

Erik crossed the threshold of Chase Manor and winced at the pointed look Harper was spearing into him. No one liked when their boss gave you the evil eye. When your boss tasked you with a job and you failed at the first hurdle—well, that didn't sit right at all.

"Sorry, there was a problem at HQ."

Harper was five feet one and a half and looked like she would fall over on those spindly heels if you pushed her gently with a finger. Yet somehow she managed to manhandle all two hundred and twenty three pounds of him into a small room—or large closet, depending on your point of view—off the main entrance. The door remained ajar, though it might have been better if it had fully closed. He wouldn't mind if Harper's feral expression wasn't quite so clear.

"Does that problem have dark curly hair, lovely blue eyes, and no love for a certain Swedish goaltender?"

"Uh, possibly. We got stuck in the elevator—all fixed—

but she left in a hurry. I tried chasing her down but she was pretty fast."

"Well, speed isn't what I pay you for, Fish." She tapped a foot. "Any idea why she blew in here about five minutes ago looking like the Ghost of Christmas Pucked?"

"I need to talk to her." He still couldn't believe it. *You fucked me and forgot.*

The thing is, he did remember. The night. The girl. The sex.

The great sex.

He had been drinking, but that wasn't the problem. She gave him her number—on a napkin—and he had put it in his pocket or at least he thought he had before they headed to his place.

She had stayed over. Ridden his cock like a rodeo queen then lay back and let him taste her. Everywhere. He remembered all that gorgeous red hair laid out on his pillow.

But Casey was a brunette with wild curls. The woman he remembered had smooth, straight, flowing hair the color of October leaves in his hometown of Ö-vik. The next morning she was gone before he woke up and that damn napkin was nowhere to be found.

No wonder Casey was furious with him. When he met her again, it didn't register that they were the same person.

Harper was looking at him, those green eyes slits of death. She poked a finger in his chest, more of an upward jab because he was so much taller than her.

"What did you do?"

"Nothing. Well, something, which was fine"—more than fine, the sex had been phenomenal—"and then nothing, which wasn't fine."

"What the hell does that mean? Is that some Swedish proverb?"

He couldn't fess up to Harper. She'd strip him naked, bind his wrists, ankles, and balls with stick tape, and leave him to die in the middle of the practice rink.

Not even the regular rink.

"I'm going to fix it."

Her eyes went wide. "Erik, did you hurt my executive assistant?"

"Thought she was your personal assistant."

"I just gave her a promotion because I've a feeling she deserves it for whatever she's had to put up with for the last year. Every time she had to look at your too-fucking-handsome face—"

"You don't even know what I did!"

"But it was something. Tell me!"

"Minou." A deep rumble echoed on the other side of the door before it was pushed open to let in more life-affirming light from the hallway and a shot at Erik making it out alive. He had never been so glad to see his former teammate Remy DuPre, husband of the woman before him.

"Anything I need to worry about?" the honey-voiced Cajun murmured with a lot more calmness than the situation deserved. Erik was about to be spit-roasted here.

"I've got it under control," Harper said in that steely tone she used whenever someone on the team fucked up majorly or worse, disappointed her. "Jorgenson was just about to tell me what he did to kill the light in Casey's eyes."

Remy stood at the door, arms folded, looking mildly sympathetic to Erik's plight. "Sounds a bit dramatic."

She hitched an eyebrow. "Erik?"

"It's between me and her."

Harper tried to kill him right then with her eyes like cut emeralds. Or maybe cut emeralds with spiky edges dripped in ... poison? Yeah, poison. Erik was sure she would have added her fists if Remy hadn't stepped inside and curled an arm around her waist.

"Let the boy make it right."

"You'd better." One final finger poke in the pec and then he was alone, wondering how the hell he was going to fix this mess.

"Hey, you okay?"

Casey turned to find Mia Wallace with her head cocked in concern. Mia was hockey royalty: sister to Vadim Petrov, the Rebels captain, girlfriend of Rebels center Cal Foreman, and a talented player heading for the Olympics in February. They had hung out together during some of the Rebels games and clicked, so it was nice to have someone to chat with at this party.

If only she wasn't so unnerved by what had happened.

"Yeah, fine. The elevator got stuck at work and it sort of freaked me out."

"Oh, no, that's terrifying!"

More terrifying was having to spend time in an enclosed space with Erik. She hadn't meant to blurt out their connection like that—she had a most excellent plan to take it to the grave—but he had pushed. Right after he soothed her silly fears about the cable snapping and the car plummeting three floors to kill them both. They would have found her covered in twisted metal, pretzeled around the Rebels goalie.

He had goaded her to reveal the truth. Or maybe she was overstating that. Maybe she had been ready to speak it after all this time. She wanted to see the horror float across his face. For a guy who came across as clueless, he was surprisingly bossy.

It turned her on.

Which made her the most pathetic woman in the room.

"It was a bit scary but I'm fine. Really."

Tara Becker, Mia's friend, appeared. "What's going on?"

"Casey got stuck in the elevator at Rebels HQ."

"Oh, God, are you okay?"

"I'm fine. It was just for a couple of minutes and it was over before I knew what had hit me. Just a shock." Which was pretty much Erik's reaction when she dropped that knowledge on him. Flummoxed. Like she had ripped the elevator floor from under him.

Harper was making a toast, welcoming the new players and congratulating everyone on the decent run for the season so far. She introduced Hale Fitzgerald, the new general manager, who added a few words of his own.

Casey had already met him when he came in to interview. A native of Georgia, Fitz was older, maybe early forties, but still clearly in great shape. That accent was to die for as well, thick and syrupy with just the right amount of silky edge to it. With the toasts done, Casey turned to Mia and Tara.

"He's got big shoes to fill," she murmured. "People really miss Dante." Their previous GM had retired to become a stay-at-home dad to Rosie, his little girl with Cade Burnett.

"I miss looking at him," Tara said, sipping her wine. "I know he's gay but that guy was one fine piece. Now we've got this geriatric geezer in, which is not an adequate substitute. Where can I lodge a complaint?"

"Uh …" Mia bit her lip and gave an awkward smile over Tara's shoulder.

Hale walked by, his mouth quirked. "Ladies."

Tara blinked and colored, watching as Hale moved smoothly through the room, shaking hands with the players and front office staff. "Thanks for the heads-up, Wallace."

Mia gave a finger jab in Tara's direction. "That's all on you. Maybe think about turning on the filter between your brain and mouth before you blab your opinions on the Rebel chief executives."

Tara shook her head in disgust and turned back to Casey. "Were you alone?"

"What?"

"In the elevator. That's a great way to get up close and personal with a guy. Maybe I should add it to my strategy list."

Tara's strategy list was all part of her grand scheme to score a pro-athlete. According to Mia, she had binders. Man binders.

Casey would rather not get into her solo or not status in the elevator, and luckily she didn't have to. The air had changed, like the molecules suddenly tingled with electricity. She looked toward the entrance to the room—the salon, Harper called it—and sure enough, the man himself had arrived.

God, he looked good.

Now she was acting as if she hadn't already been confronted with Erik in all his blond-haired, blue-eyed, Nordic gorgeousness.

You've already seen him back at Rebels HQ. Better yet, you already looked right into those gorgeous eyes and got a whiff of his aftershave and felt him deep inside you.

Her entire body was an electric current, live with want and self-disgust. What kind of woman was attracted to a man who had cast her aside, who couldn't even recall her face when he met her again? At least Andrew had wanted her enough to be willing to try again, though really he needed a doormat to wipe his shoes on while he ascended the throne. Clearly, she wasn't the kind of woman who inspired a deeper connection.

Erik was coming over, a palpable intensity driving every step.

"I need a drink!" She gushed to Mia and Tara. "Do you need a drink?"

Mia opened her mouth but Casey was already backing away. "Of course you do! I'll bring you something."

She scrabbled her way to the kitchen, expecting it would be busy with catering people but not at all. Only Remy DuPre and Reid Durand, one of the Rebels players, heads close together in what was obviously a serious conversation.

"Oh, sorry, I didn't realize anyone was in here."

"Pas de probleme," Remy said in that distinctive Cajun drawl.

Casey turned and crashed into Erik. She jumped back and held up her hands. Overdramatic, perhaps, but she was in a full-scale panic here.

"So that's it?" Erik said. "We're not even going to talk about it?"

"I have nothing to say to you."

Oh God, the expression on his face ... she had really hurt him.

But he hurt her first.

He might not have meant to. He was merely an inconsiderate jock who fucked random women and didn't remember. While she wasn't sure if that was worse than the knife in her back wielded by Andrew, she couldn't help how she felt.

Discarded. Used.

She headed out to the hallway, thankful he didn't follow her. Glad that he was finally respecting her boundaries.

Only now it was no longer a festering secret in her heart, she wondered if maybe they *should* talk it out. It might be amusing to listen to his excuses, his sad efforts to come up with a reason why she had never stood out to him and was just another in a revolving door of women through his pro-athlete bed.

Not tonight, though. She needed to process it, maybe talk to her cat about next steps.

No one would notice if she left. Harper might ask her tomorrow if she had enjoyed the party, except tomorrow was Christmas Eve and the front office was closed until the twenty-seventh. Three days to binge Netflix and knock back eggnog and sit around in PJs.

Alone, but she would Skype with her parents on Christmas Day. It wouldn't be so terrible.

Theo Kershaw emerged from the salon, a big grin on his face. "Hey, Casey, happy holidays!"

"You, too!" Theo was one of the nicest guys on the team, a recent father with a cute three-month-old baby boy. "How's Hatch?"

"Home with the babysitter giving her hell, I imagine. I'm trying to get Ellie to let her hair down but she hates leaving him. Have you seen the latest pics?" Without waiting for her response, the proud papa extracted his phone and pulled up a gallery of photos. "Here he is in a Rebels onesie. And here he is with a candy cane, which means he'll have no problem with a hockey stick. Look at that handling!"

"Aw, he's a natural! And his hair is fuller than when you brought him by before."

"Yeah." He touched his own finely-coiffed do. "Lustrous like his dad."

"I'd expect nothing less."

After a couple more swipes and the requisite cooing from her side, he asked, "Hey, have you seen Durand?"

"In the kitchen."

Grinning his leave, he went on his way. The last year had seen several of the players find *the one* and settle down, including Theo, Levi Hunt, Gunnar Bond, and Cal Foreman. Cade and Dante had welcomed a baby girl and Bren St. James and his wife Violet were expecting their first child. For all the bad rep that hockey players got, some of them were built for the long haul. If she was feeling optimistic about the state of love, that might have given her hope. *If.*

She opened the hallway closet, a giant walk-in, and stepped inside. Where was her coat? She'd handed it off to Harper who must have—oh, there it was at the back. Just as she went to grab it, the door closed behind her, shrouding her in darkness.

She squealed. It was a little too close for comfort given her elevator-to-hell experience earlier.

"Hey, it's okay," a smooth voice said. A smooth, accented voice.

"What are you doing?"

She knew what he was doing, but it was dark, and she did not want to be in another tight space with Erik Jorgenson.

"Casey, we need to talk."

5

"I've already told you I won't be talking about it." She fumbled for her coat, just as a pool of light hit the ceiling. Erik was holding his phone with the light on, but facing up like a lamp. He placed it on a shelf, positioned so it gave the closet an eerie, campfire glow.

Like they were about to tell ghost stories.

Well, she had one. *Once a girl met a guy who gave her the best night of her life, completely* ghosted *her (get it?), then compounded her misery by not recognizing her when she ran into him years later.*

"You blindsided me, Casey. You dropped this knowledge and then ran out of Rebels HQ, leaving me with my jaw on the floor. Not cool. And now I've got Harper sticking pins in my voodoo doll and wishing very evil things would happen to me."

What did Harper have to do with this? He'd better not have told her.

That thought had barely formed when she found the space shrink to virtually nothing. She could smell his aftershave, combined with something uniquely Erik. He was close, tall, all-consuming. With that light above his head, he looked like a fallen angel.

Something softened inside her. Not her heart, unless it had relocated to below her waist.

"I remember that night," he murmured, all husky and seductive.

"No, you don't," she whispered. "If you did, you wouldn't have ignored me."

I won't be ignored, Dan! Now she was quoting Glenn Close from *Fatal Attraction*. One boiled bunny coming right up.

"Casey—"

"It's okay." She had to forgive him—or some version of it—and move on. Otherwise it would be between them forever and she liked her job. Better to get it over with, if only so she could get out of this closet with some dignity.

Yet as the words bubbled in her throat, struggling for a shape that wouldn't sound pitiful, she found herself itching to reveal some fraction of the pain. The heartache. Make him understand that it was more than just a night of hot sex.

"I didn't expect you to call me—I mean, why would you? You're a hotshot pro-hockey star and I'm just some random girl in a bar. I went about my business and lived my life, keeping that night in here." She touched her heart with a trembling hand. "Because it was a nice thing to happen to me. A nice thing before ..." She shook her head as another potent memory took over. Andrew and Melanie, the woman he had dumped her for. The new model: better, brighter, built to last, or at least put him on the partnership track. "I watched your games with this secret knowledge that I had about you. And me, I suppose. But it faded over time. I was long over it. One-night stand, no big deal."

"Casey, I—"

She did a zip it move with her hands, needing him to be quiet. Needing this moment to speak her truth without his excuses steamrolling her.

"But then I started working for Harper and I thought, oh, that's nice, I'll run into Erik Jorgenson again and it might be a bit awkward but so what? We'll laugh about it and that will be that. Only you didn't recognize me. Not even a glimmer."

It was embarrassing to admit it had meant so much to her. After all, a month later, Andrew had come crawling back saying he had made a huge mistake and she was the one for him. The one he needed at his back as he finished law school. She had stashed the night with Erik in her heart's attic and thought of it with a what-if fondness as the cobwebs spun the silk of time around them. She was meant for a real relationship, not a fantasy.

But her reality eventually became a nightmare and the fantasy wasn't much better.

Erik was breathing hard, an agitation in him she would never have expected.

"I didn't recognize you, I admit that. It's been something like seven years and you had different hair then. Red, smooth, glossy. I remember it spread out on my pillow, this beautiful waterfall of color as I fucked you."

She let out a small sound of surprise, maybe because he combined that image of her lying beneath him with the crude essentialism of what that night was about. An amazing release, a fuck for the ages. Yet she sensed he wasn't trying to diminish it. Back then he had moved inside her, reaching so deep she thought she'd never feel that good again.

She hadn't, which was so unfair.

What he said about her hair ... sure it had looked different, but was it that much of a stretch? Was that why he didn't recognize her all these years later?

No, she refused to let him off the hook so easily. Of course she wouldn't be memorable enough to stand out. He hadn't even tried to contact her.

"You never called me."

"I lost your number."

"What?"

"You wrote it on a napkin at the Empty Net but I couldn't find it. I thought it was in my pocket only it wasn't. I searched my apartment high and low, and couldn't find it. I remember we talked about home and living in a new place and *The Office*. You loved that show and I hadn't seen it but you kept telling me I had to watch it." His brow furrowed. "You wouldn't tell me your name."

"Th-that's not right." *Hold up.* Doubts snuck in. He remembered details about that night yet he couldn't remember *her*? And not telling him her name? None of this made any sense.

"Yes, I kept asking but you said you wanted to be someone else that night. And then you said I should call you …"

"Coco." They both said it at the same time and her hand flew to her mouth in shock. She had forgotten that. The silly name, the number on the napkin, the red hair.

All she had remembered was the great sex and the hurt feelings when he didn't call.

Then seven years later, the hurt coming back for a boomerang whammy to scoop out her chest cavity when she met his gaze in the Rebels' front office, only to find it curious but unknowing.

He inhaled a deep breath. "I'm sorry, Casey. You're right to be pissed off. I'm a jerk."

She swallowed hard. He *was* a jerk, wasn't he? She had invested a lot of time and energy into thinking so. First for ghosting her, then for blanking her. She wasn't ready to give up on the feeling. A girl needed something to keep her warm, even if it was righteous anger at a man.

"Well, now you know." She sounded so starchy. When had she become this person?

"Now I know." He loomed over her. Even with her heels, he had to be at least eight inches taller than her. "So what are we going to do about it?"

His voice was different. Not apologetic, but more assured. Erik Jorgenson thought they were over the hump.

"About what?"

"The fact that we've made up. We are no longer enemies, though I'm not sure if people can be enemies if only one person knows *why* they are enemies—"

"No." She put a hand on his chest, which felt like a plate of armor. A warm, breathing, sexy plate of armor.

It also felt like a mistake.

The best kind, a voice whispered.

"No?" he prompted.

"I'll tell you what will happen. I won't give you the evil eye the next time you're at Rebels HQ and you can stop trying to talk to me. Because now you know and we can move on."

He snorted. "Not sure I know anything except that you're still mad at me."

"It doesn't just go away because it's out there."

"But it's good to clear the air, yes? I'm not used to people being mad at me unless they're wearing blades and padding."

The air was anything but clear. It was thick, charged, sentient. Alive with potential.

Sexy potential.

"I'm sorry if I came off as unprofessional." *Ms. Prissy, come on down.* "I'll do my best to keep all future interactions on an even keel."

"Casey, it's okay. You have every right to be angry and if you need to continue with that, then fine. Take the time you need."

Okay, more mature than she expected.

"Unless you don't need time."

And we're back. "Excuse me?"

His hand covered hers, which somehow had remained on his chest during the last sixty seconds. She had left it there because she needed an anchor and he was the closest thing to ballast in this closet.

"Unless you want to move to the apology acceptance part of the process."

"I already told you that the feeling doesn't just go away."

He rubbed a thumb over the pulse point of her wrist, such an intimate gesture. But then this whole experience was a bubble of intimacy in the most unexpected place.

"But how can I make it go away? How can I make up for it, Casey?"

The way he said her name had her regretting not giving it to him all those years ago. She would have liked to hear it from his lips as he thrust inside her …

No. Her brain would not be making that trip. It would not be thinking of how he could make the pain go away with his hands in places she had dreamed of for too many lonely nights since that one special time. It would not be thinking of how this man could make it up to her with his body rocking into hers, taking her down memory lane, but only the good parts. It would not be thinking of going home alone to her cat and her PJs and more Chex mix than was good for a one hundred and fifty pound woman.

"You-you can't." Her words were uncertain, her voice timid.

He raised their joined hands to his lips and placed a kiss on her palm. It was really too sweet for the moment, for this space, for all the dark thoughts she had about him.

The revenge she wanted.

Oh, yes. That felt good. The idea of it, the surge she needed.

"You sure?" He was doing an excellent job of not crowding her even though he was inches away from her. Assuring her she was in control. This was her circus. "I can't make you forget about it?" His lips were close to hers, all she had to do was take another round of the pleasure she'd been seeking that night she went into the Empty Net and bagged herself a hockey player.

"I don't want to forget about it," she whispered, not because she wanted to hold onto the hate. It was the best night of her life. So it was nothing to him, just another fangirl in a bar. But it had meant something to her and even with the pain, it *still* meant something to her.

How ludicrous to give that night, this man, the moment, such power. But there it was.

She wanted to feel that again—and his mouth was right there. More than that, his heart was beating and his eyes, those Nordic blues, were pinpricks. He wanted her.

She had power in *this* moment.

"Apologize," she murmured.

"I'm—"

She put a finger to his lips. "Not with words." She traced his bottom lip, full and unbelievably sensual, and moved her hand to his jaw. He usually had a trim beard during the regular season, and it always looked so good on him. Now she let her fingertips enjoy the sensation of that rough facial hair.

Pulling their joined hands down to her side, he took another step in and cupped her hip with his free hand. Extended the fingers of that hand so it dug into the flesh at the top of her ass. It felt good.

Physical. *Dirty.*

When he pulled her toward him so their chests met and his mouth was half an inch from hers, it felt even better.

No words. She was tired of smooth talkers, men with weak excuses and false praise.

Tell me with your hands that you want me.

Tell me with your kisses that you desire me.

Tell me with no words because I won't believe you anyway.

His lips brushed tentatively against hers, testing, teasing. She made a sound of frustration, but probably something closer to anticipation.

"I got you," he whispered.

"Shut up," she growled right back because she wanted to be got.

Then he shut *her* up, just like that, with his mouth where she needed it. Giving it good and taking her anger. Shaping and smoothing it to sweetness, when sweetness was a thing she knew nothing of.

Not anymore.

6

Angry women were not usually his jam.

Erik liked cheerful, pliant partners, sort of like him. He was usually good-humored and easygoing, and that was what he was drawn to in a mate.

Not that he'd ever had a mate.

He was beginning to think there was a reason for that. This woman had pointed out a problem—his absolute cluelessness.

So there was a reason for it. A very good reason. Only he couldn't exactly explain that to her because it sounded absurd. How do you tell a woman that her hair made an impression but her face is forgettable?

No, Casey wasn't like him. Not easygoing. Not accepting. And she had every reason to be this way. She was incensed and hurt.

He would make it better. If it was the last thing he ever did before his punctured body—Harper's voodoo doll, remember?—was found in some ditch, this was what he would do.

Give Casey her revenge.

She wanted to use him. Punish him. That was okay. He would happily bear the brunt of her pain. He was used to pucks raining down on him and he had good padding, both on the ice and in his heart. He had been brought up surrounded by love, supported by a family who sheltered and protected him. He could do this for her. She wouldn't hurt him, no matter how much she tried.

But if it made her feel better, he would let her think she had.

"Shut up," she said again, though he hadn't said anything, just moved his lips back an inch. She probably thought he was about to speak and ruin it and she was having none of it.

"Hmm," he hummed, and that sound sent a corresponding vibration through her body. She shuddered in his arms and he took this as a sign he should keep her warm, wrap her up, and that involved a deeper push into the closet.

His hand had been gripping her hip but now he flexed it, moved it to under her ass and cupped.

Oh yeah.

She had a great ass, a full, sweet curve that fit his palm perfectly especially when he squeezed and pulled her in a seal against his dick.

Christ. She shivered again and released a breathy moan. No longer an invitation, this was a demand, and he grasped the crease between buttock and thigh and hitched her up. Parting her legs so he could step into their embrace and ...

Rub. A good, dirty rub against her heat.

The dress fabric was in the way but not for long. He rolled it to the top of her thighs, then realized his mistake.

"Is this o—"

"No."

He froze.

"I mean, no talking," she panted, before moving her hands beneath his jacket over his chest and around to his back. Sealing him closer.

She didn't want to hear him. He should be hurt that his words, his voice, the products of his mind should be so offensive to her. He had done her wrong as his friend, defenseman Cade Burnett, would say. And now he would do her right.

No words, just actions. They spoke louder, yes?

He could kiss her all day, the taste of her was so sweet. He bet she tasted good everywhere. He wanted to know.

He needed to know.

He fell to his knees, a familiar position for him. In the goal, he lived his life in a crouch. Ready to deflect and defend, always keeping his eye on the puck. On his knees, he did his best work.

Applying his mouth to the soft skin inside her thigh, he felt her shiver of appreciation. He would assume she would push him away if this bothered her. But he didn't like to assume—he wanted enthusiastic agreement.

He leaned back, looked up with his hands still behind her thighs, and waited. Having made a career of waiting, it was something he excelled at.

He would give her a moment to breathe. To think. To regret.

The light from his phone cast a pool on the closet's ceiling, like a Nordic sun suspending the day. But her face was still in shadow so he couldn't tell what she was thinking.

Until she curled a soft hand around his jaw and whispered, "Yes."

The most beautiful word in the world.

He moved his thumbs inside her thighs and nudged them apart, while at the same time ensuring her skirt rolled up a few more inches. It released her arousal and his subsequent moan.

She shivered again as his thumbs traveled north and grazed her panties. Hot, fragrant, Christ. His mouth targeted that silky triangle and latched on, sucking through to make what was damp, wet.

Her moan filled the space, and then her hand urged his forward, and soon *his* hands were pulling those panties halfway down her thighs. But not all the way. He liked the look of them, the sleazy vision they created in the half-dark. He liked how, as his tongue dipped between her legs, she was restrained from spreading wider. That shouldn't be good, but it added a layer of frustration, of additional need to this moment.

He would work to get her off.

Find pleasure in the exploration.

Slake his thirst on the nectar he would find here.

"Oh God oh God," she moaned as his tongue delved deeper, through those slippery folds, into the heart of her. She opened right up for him, vulnerable and trusting. He drank her down, loving how she had started to shake, not just her thighs but her entire body.

She squeezed his neck and went completely still, but he didn't stop, just continued to suck. Feast. She was right there on the edge of reason, and then she broke in a surge against his mouth. He was so turned on, hard as a puck, in pain, to be truthful. But he continued to suckle, gently, to keep the pleasure front and center and minimize her sensitivity.

Her body softened, slumped, and her hand in his hair loosened its grip.

Fell away.

She was back from wherever he'd sent her, returning to an awareness of what happened. Of who he was.

The man she despised.

He could let her off the hook, pull back and give her space, but no. He wanted her to make a choice.

When she didn't immediately withdraw, he took it as a sign. Maybe she was still in a fuck-daze or maybe she was feeling awkward and unsure how to return to the time before.

He wasn't unsure.

He had never been more certain of a mission in all his life. Det är saligare att giva än att taga. *It was more blissful to give than to receive.*

His lips were wet, his beard damp with her pleasure, his dick about to explode—and he started to lick again. She jerked, surprised, but she didn't pull away. This might be his only chance with her and he would take it. Own this moment as she owned him. He would give her another night to remember, one that left her in no doubt about how good they could be together.

It only took a minute for her to start rocking into his mouth, taking this pleasure as her right. As what she deserved after being dismissed by some hockey bro douchebag. (That would be him.) He wished it lasted longer but it was something he would take with him, a memory to fuel fantasy moments later.

This was the last time she would let him touch her. Of that he was certain.

She cried out, just as two things happened:

Light streamed in because someone had opened the door.

That same someone said, "Shit. Sorry!" and shut it quickly. Fucking Kershaw.

Erik sat back and wiped his mouth. "You okay, Casey?"

Hastily, she pulled her panties up before he had a

chance to help, her dress down before he had a chance to memorize that treasure between her thighs.

As he stood, she turned away from him and grabbed at the coats behind her.

"Casey, are you okay?"

"Fine!" then quieter, "Absolutely fine. I need to leave."

"I'll take you home."

"No!" She grabbed a coat and turned, blinking in what he assumed was annoyance that he was still here. "I'll grab an Uber."

Because he stood in her way, she turned her back and struggled into her coat. The collar was folded in on itself so he unflipped it, leaving him to think on what it would be like to have access to her collar every day. To be able to do that one little thing for her as she got ready in the morning, heading into work, as they kissed their goodbyes at the door.

The yearning almost made him buckle.

She pivoted quickly.

"We're going to forget that ever happened."

"Nope."

She stared at him. "Nope?"

"You can't police my thoughts. If I want to remember it, think about it, fantasize about it when I get off, then I'll do so. And you know something, Casey?" He leaned in close enough to see her blue eyes wide and fired up. "You won't be forgetting about this anytime soon, either."

She shook her head, though not in denial. She couldn't deny that she would be remembering this forever. No, she was mad as hell. "I need to leave."

"Sure. I'll be in touch."

Those eyes went even wider. "You will not!"

He stepped aside but the space was tight and he was big. It wasn't his fault she had to brush by him, her hip glancing off his erection, the one that was in no danger of subsiding. Perhaps it was better she was leaving—he really needed to do something about this hard-on.

"Good night, Coco."

"What—oh, forget it."

She left and he let her, knowing they weren't finished. Knowing they had barely begun.

7

Casey awoke to the sound of a jet engine coming in for a landing close to her ear.

"Keanu, what have I told you about waking me up?"

Her black and white cat—her fat black and white cat—left off his noisy purr to sniff, then sneeze in her face.

"Happy Christmas Eve to you, too."

She checked her phone. Her parents had already texted to say they would be out of range during the cruise today but they would check in tomorrow to wish her a great holiday. They also advised her that the Wi-Fi was spotty and they were really quite busy, so if they didn't call, don't be surprised.

Her parents exhausted her.

It was a little unsettling to be spending Christmas alone. Last year, they'd made more of an effort to include her because she had just broken up with Andrew. Unfortunately they had loved her ex and there was always a hint of censure about her reaction to his betrayal. She should have done more, as if putting the man through law school and working her ass off to support him on her salary wasn't enough.

Finding text messages between your boyfriend of eight years and his co-worker, expressing how Casey had "outlived her usefulness" had been unexpected. She had always known that Andrew never thought of her as his equal, but it still surprised her to see it laid out so callously. She wasn't polished or driven enough. What was it he had said to Melanie in one of those exchanges?

I could never be serious about a woman who lets me walk all over her.

Like their eight years together had merely been a stopgap, with Casey as the placeholder. Her emotional and financial support of him, her efforts to be the woman behind the great man, had been a tick in the con column. He despised her for her kindness.

Usually at this point in the mental self-flagellation she would be checking his Facebook feed to see what he was up to. This morning? She had no desire to go down that thorny path.

Was it possible she had pushed through to the other side and was finally numb to the pain? Some sort of grieving process was at work here.

New me jumpstarted by orgasms.

She sat up in bed, an image of Erik on his knees before her in that closet returning unbidden—okay, bidden, very much bidden—to her mind. Was this the answer? Losing herself in bone-melting sex?

From the moment she entered that elevator to the moment she awoke ten minutes ago, she had only thought of that glorious Swede. (No doubt he figured substantially in her dreams even if she couldn't remember the exact details.)

His ridiculously handsome jaw, dusted with facial hair that had felt like a dream against her thighs.

His Arctic-blue eyes that had shown genuine remorse on

hearing her painful recounting of how much that night had meant to her.

His tongue as it made all the sorrow vanish, if only for a few moments.

Andrew had left her brain because Erik was there to replace him, a conclusion she did not enjoy nearly as much as she should have. She didn't want to substitute one selfish man for another, not even one so generous in the oral department. (Andrew was never a fan, which should have told her all she needed to know.)

Erik had definitely served a purpose. She wouldn't say he'd made up for his failings exactly, more like her heart had softened toward him. Not quite ready to forgive, she might have graduated to understanding his behavior all those years ago and then again, when they "reunited." Some of the blame could be on her side: she never gave her real name, she had been a redhead that one night, and maybe he had lost her number on that napkin. She recalled now that she'd offered it after he asked, even though his initial request had been to put his number in her phone contacts. But she had resisted that. It placed the burden on her to call him and she didn't think she'd ever be brave enough.

A perfect storm of puzzle pieces that might explain away his behavior. Or perhaps she was reaching for a tidy explanation to make herself feel better about getting busy with the guy again.

Forgiveness shouldn't come so easily, but the next time she saw him, she would be less standoffish. Besides they had renewed history. It was pretty hard to act like a raging bitch when a man had made you come twice in a closet at your boss's house during a team holiday party.

She clapped her hand over her mouth.

She had done that! Left him hard and aching, too—

she'd definitely encountered his "problem" on the way out of the closet and she wasn't sorry for it. Not one bit.

Score one for the sisterhood. Or maybe two because it had happened twice.

"Well, Keanu," she said to her suspicious kitty, "maybe your human is back."

An hour later, Casey was second-guessing her *go girl* talk as she stared at the delivery that graced her coffee table.

A poinsettia.

A man had delivered it about five minutes ago, and despite Casey's love of poinsettias, she was now viewing it like it was a Venus flytrap.

The card with it read: *Thanks for coming at the party last night. God Jul, Erik.*

Hmm. She looked up "God Jul": it meant Good Yule or Merry Christmas in Swedish.

But that wasn't why she was staring at the plant like it had offended her ancestors. Oh, no. It was the "at" in that sentence. Not "thanks for coming *to* the party" but "thanks for coming *at* the party."

Erik's English was fine and that preposition choice was no mistake. He was thanking her for … coming!

How could she enjoy her victory for the sisterhood when he was undermining it with his perfect English, cheery holiday plant, and well wishes for her sexual health? Thanks for coming, indeed!

She opened her phone contacts and scrolled to his number. As assistant to the CEO, she had all the players' contact information. She could text him and thank him for the gift. It was the polite thing to do. Though she wouldn't really be thanking him. She would be doing it to pick a fight, which would be better in person.

She tapped his number.

He answered on the first ring.

"Hello, Casey."

That voice. She loved it, how deliberate his pronunciation was. His English back then hadn't been quite as good, but now it was perfect—and perfectly able to send her into a tailspin.

She also remembered how it once coaxed her to do hot, wicked things, only back then he'd called her Coco, a fact she had forgotten until last night. How strange that he remembered these details—her fake name, her fake hair, her fake persona. Even that they had talked about her favorite show, *The Office*. Was it possible that night had meant something to him after all, that she had made as much of an impression on him as he on her?

"How did you know it was me?"

"You've sent texts to the team before about travel arrangements and the like."

She had. For a split second she'd forgotten one of her primary duties. This was the downside of orgasms; not only did you forget the worm who dumped you, you also forgot the rudimentary elements of your job.

He went on. "Did you get the julstjärna?"

"Is that the plant?"

"Yes, that's what we call it in Sweden. It means Christmas tree star."

Oh, something inside her warmed at that and a couple of chips of ice fell away from the fortress surrounding her heart. She coughed, aiming to restore its regular rhythm. "Right, that's what I'm calling about. It was really not necessary—"

"Do you like it?"

She swallowed. His voice was low, smoky, and doing things to her. Again.

"I do. Thank you. But you shouldn't have."

"I was a little worried you might be going out of town but Harper assured me you weren't."

Harper again. The woman had no right to interfere like this.

"I would usually be spending it with my"—*boyfriend*—"parents but they're out of town." In case that sounded too pathetic, she quickly added, "But I'll head over to Bren and Violet's tomorrow for the Orphan Christmas."

Not pathetic at all!

"I'll also be an orphan, so I will see you there. Shall we say noon in the closet?"

"Erik—"

"Too soon?" He sounded amused, which reminded her that she had things to say.

"About what happened."

"In the closet or all those years ago?"

"In the—what about all those years ago?"

"I don't think we have put that to bed, have we?"

She battled a smile. Lost the fight. This was the boy—the man—she remembered from that night in the Empty Net. He had charmed her with his goofiness and she had been swept off her feet into another world where she felt adored.

Of course she had been ripe for it. Recently dumped, desperate for a boost to her self-confidence. She got a hot night and was still greedy for more. Only Erik never called and Andrew sauntered back into her life. She hated the what-if game but she couldn't help herself.

She knew better now than to believe any word out of a

man's mouth. Yet she realized that Erik might not be completely at fault here.

"There's nothing more to say about it. I may have been a little ... harsh on you. After all, I did look different and I used a fake name."

"Yes, but I should have—" He checked his speech and blew out an exasperated breath. He should have what? Remembered her?

He went on. "I lost your number. The bar staff didn't know who you were and—"

"The bar staff? At the Empty Net?"

"Yes. I tried to describe you but they didn't remember. And there I was thinking they would all recall the beautiful woman a hockey superstar goaltender was flirting with all night. I guess I wasn't quite the center of the universe I thought. It was a harsh lesson."

Do. Not. Smile. "I can't believe you went in looking for me." Not sure she believed it now.

"I thought maybe I lost the napkin there, though I was so certain I'd put it in my pocket before we left the bar. The staff were useless. No information and I never found my Coco, until now."

Her breath hitched. *My Coco.*

"That's not my name."

"I like both your names, but Coco has a certain style, I have to say."

She giggled then slapped a guilty hand over her mouth. Keanu sent an accusing glare her way, so she scowled back at him. He knew nothing.

"You're such a goof."

"That's what people think, I suppose."

She didn't mean to imply that was all there was to him. For fuck's sake, was she starting to empathize with the man?

No no no.

She needed to wrap this up before she melted into a puddle of complete forgiveness. Struggling for a businesslike tone, she said, "I just wanted to say thank you. For the plant and for …"

"For?"

"For being so calm in the elevator. Not my finest moment but you were on hand to help me get a grip."

"And …"

Oh, he was a saucy one. She would not thank him for the orgasms. He owed her.

"And have a pleasant Christmas Eve."

"Julafton."

"What did you just call me?"

He chuckled, a graveled sound that sent shivers of pleasure down her spine. "Julafton. That's Christmas Eve in Sweden. In fact …" He paused, and her heart stuttered in anticipation. "Would you like to come over for lunch?"

"Lunch?"

"I'm cooking the julmat. That's the special meal we have today, which is the traditional celebration of Yule in Sweden. I won't be there with my family. I always miss it, but I usually cook some of the dishes."

"For yourself?"

"And for the guys on the team, but none of them are around this year. They are all paired off, making babies, forging ahead with their lives."

There was that hint of melancholy again. She understood it. "I was just thinking that last night, how so many of the team have found their mates and have families now." She had expected she herself would be well on her way, maybe a kid under her belt by now. But Andrew had other ideas. She shook her head, not wanting to dull the pleasant glow she felt while talking to Erik.

"Yes, everyone is finding their special someone," he murmured.

"We'll probably be put at the sad singles table at Bren's tomorrow."

She heard his smile. Not sure how she knew, but she did. "We could practice today."

"Eating while single?"

"Yes, I've been up since five a.m. cooking with only a break to visit the florist. It would be nicer to spend Julafton with someone. Just some food, Casey, no shenanigans."

And what if she wanted shenanigans?

She had *not* thought that. Except she had.

"Are you sure? It seems like a special meal."

"It is. And now it will be more special because you're here."

She closed her eyes against the little sparks of joy those words ignited.

"I can't really leave my cat. He needs medication on a certain schedule." Usually she drove home over her lunch break to take care of him.

"Bring your cat if he doesn't mind traveling."

"Well, he does mind but he's not the boss of me."

Erik chuckled. "I'm going to guess that you're being sarcastic and that your cat probably *is* the boss of you. Cats always are." He had her there. "So what do you say?"

Be brave. "Okay. When?"

"Come over whenever you're ready. Do you know where I live?"

She did, and not only because she was assistant to the CEO. Curious, she had driven by his place once. He had graduated to a really nice townhouse in Riverbrook, not the usual sprawling pro-athlete McMansion but definitely a lot of square footage for a single guy.

But she couldn't say that. Instead she feigned ignorance.

"Text me your address."

"Sure. See you soon, Coco."

8

Erik placed the last plate on the table and grimaced.

It might be a bit much.

Usually he would have a few of the guys over for Christmas Eve lunch, though each year he'd lived in Riverbrook, just north of Chicago, the numbers had dwindled as his friends found love. This year, Theo had invited him to Saugatuck to spend the holiday with Elle, Hatch, and his grandmother, but Erik hadn't taken him up on it. Theo was a family man now, just like Remy, Cade, Ford, Bren, and so many others. Most of the guys were hitched and happy.

It was enough to make a guy feel lonely.

He tried not to let it bother him. After all, he had a job he loved, amazing friends, a family he got along with—might have helped that they lived in Sweden, his sisters were nightmares walking—and plenty of people who told him he was a good guy. But he hadn't connected with anyone special except for that one time seven years ago. When it came down to the wire, he wasn't the kind of man a girl chose, not when there were other guys who made more of an impression.

Now there was this business with Casey. He had really fucked up there; no wonder she was so pissed at him. If anything, Erik deserved her censure.

Of course, technically he had a good reason for not recognizing her, but it would be pointless to share it now that he had somehow made it back into her good graces. He hadn't expected her to say yes to lunch. She had sounded annoyed on the phone but then he had made her laugh. Ms. Prim and Proper with her tight skirts and high heels had giggled at something stupid he said. So he went in for the kill—he had to have learned something on the ice after all these years.

His phone buzzed with a text from Theo.

> So you and Casey?

Best to play dumb.

> ??

> THEO
> You were spotted in a closet at Chase Manor.

> ERIK
> By you!

Theo sent a wink emoji.

> CAL
> WTF, Harper's assistant, Casey? With Jorgenson? That's a thing?

Fuck! Theo had put this on the team chat. Not everyone was on it—Petrov had opted out, saying as captain, he wanted to give the players space to bitch about him, which was his way of saying he expected the Rebels to talk about him constantly. Most everyone else was in the group, though ... and were all now weighing in on the Erik/Casey situation.

> **LEVI**
> Doesn't she hate you?
>
> **GUNNAR**
> Heard she ran a mile from you in the Empty Net.
>
> **KAZ**
> Like he could catch her. Good thing his job is to stay in one place on the ice.
>
> **CADE**
> Is she still mad at you? Follow up question: why was she mad at you?

Shit, this was the last thing he needed. He didn't want to embarrass Casey about how they had first met or himself about how he didn't recognize her when they met again.

> **ERIK**
> Long story. Trying to keep it on the down low.
>
> **THEO**
> Yeah, you were getting pretty down and low in that closet. She didn't *sound* mad.
>
> **ERIK**
> The next person to make a joke about this will be forced to eat Surströmming at Friday's morning skate. Don't make me bring out the stinky fish!

All quiet for a moment, then Kaz weighed in:

> Don't get your meatballs in a twist, Swede.
> Your secret's safe with me and the fifteen
> other guys on this thread. LOL.

Tate Kazminski was a notorious blabbermouth, so Erik didn't hold out much hope of discretion.

Theo sent a private message:

> Sorry, Fish. My bad.

Erik had just shot off a text telling him it was okay when the doorbell rang. His entire body vibrated with excitement. He had a quick look around. There was nothing he could do now. This was it.

No more fuckups. He wanted Casey to like him.

Because there was no doubt he liked her. Back then, the last year, now.

Before he had even opened the door, he heard a scream like the wail of a Draugen. Not human, more like—ah, Casey had brought her cat in a carrier.

She murmured soothing words, but the cat wasn't buying it. It made an unholy racket and as she calmed it, Erik took a good look at her. She wore her hair down, rich and luscious waves over her shoulders. She had that dark coat on over black pants that looked like velvet and short black boots.

"I'm sorry. I would have left him at home but he needs medication so I don't like to leave him for too long."

"It's fine. Maybe he'll be okay if you take him out of the carrier."

"Maybe." She blinked at him and bit down on her lip. With a sweeping gaze over him, he felt like he was being judged.

Which is when he realized he was wearing the holiday apron his sister Astrid had sent him with an image of a Christmas tree bauble and the words WELL HUNG in all caps. Exactly the kind of impression he didn't want to make.

"Sorry, I wasn't thinking." He pulled at the neck tie, but stopped when her small hand landed on his chest.

"No, don't. It's funny."

"Because it's true?" There he went again! Why couldn't he shut up?

His heart thumped under her fingertips and he decided he'd better get a good look at her now because there was a good chance this was it. Any second and she'd be out of here.

Feeling brave, he went for it. Placed his hand over hers and held it to his chest. Let her sense how she affected him.

She smirked. "Yeah. Because it's true."

"I've got such a bad mouth sometimes."

"You've got that right."

What? Oh, because of where his mouth ... he swallowed. Last night she had responded like a sensitive instrument to his touch. To his hands and lips. She had come on his tongue and nothing had ever tasted so good. He should know. He was a foodie.

"I'm glad you're here." Sincerity dueled with excitement in his chest.

"It was nice of you to invite me and Keanu."

Erik looked down at the carrier. "You should come in and let's get you both settled."

Another smile, bigger this time. Carrying her cat, she walked by him into the house.

∼

CASEY STEPPED inside Erik's home and got the shock of her life.

She had entered a magical Christmas wonderland.

Slowly she bent her knees and placed her bag and Keanu's carrier on the ground, for once ignoring his bad humor. Kitty would have to wait.

Her eyes roved the entrance hall—this place had a lobby!—taking it all in. The walls showcased luminous black and white photos of a trio of Swedish supermodels, just stepped off the set of *Midsommar*.

"My sisters," Erik said.

"They're beautiful."

"Doesn't make up for how annoying they are. And these are my parents, Linnea and Nils."

Casey loved that he gave pride of place to his family. It said good things about him. Her gaze greedily took in the rest. A huge tree filled a spot beside the staircase. The thing was a beast, a beautifully decorated Douglas fir beast that almost touched the ceiling.

"Wow, it's huge."

"That's what she—" He broke off, shook his head. Poor guy, trying so hard not to offend her. She pressed her lips together, hiding her urge to chuckle. "That's just for the entrance," he went on. "The one in the living room is better."

Another tree? Somebody loved Christmas.

She followed him into a lovely, warm room where an even more impressive tree filled one corner, decorated with what looked like handmade ornaments, not cheap Target tat, but painted wooden ones. She wanted to look at every single piece, touch and watch them twinkle under the lights, ask about the tales behind them because she had no doubt there were stories. From what she'd read, Christmas was a big deal in Sweden. Yet every holiday since Erik was twenty, he had spent it here because the game schedule didn't allow a long enough break for him to travel. Her heart squeezed for him.

"Is that Michael Bublé I hear?"

"It isn't Christmas until Bublé sings."

His cheeky grin made her laugh. The festive cheer didn't stop there. A roaring fire crackled in the hearth, welcoming her in to get toasty. Above it a garland-dressed mantel was topped with tons more photos, candid shots of Erik, his family, and friends. In the center, a threadbare elf eyed her warily, looking like he'd had a little too much rum-spiked eggnog.

"Your elf could do with a holiday. Or a nap."

"That's not an elf. That's Tomte."

"Tomte?" She turned to find him smiling at her, a wryness to his expression. (Erik, not the sort-of-elf. Though ...)

"Kind of like a Swedish Santa Claus."

"Like Belsnickel?"

He smiled at the reference. "Belsnickel is a warning to naughty children. Tomte is mischievous."

"So more like the elf on the shelf."

Erik shook his head, suddenly grave. "Don't let him hear you calling him that. He will play tricks on you for revenge."

Weirdly morbid.

She liked it.

"You've gone all out. It's beautiful." The walls were draped with silver-white garlands and holiday greenery. On a sideboard stood an entire Winter village. She moved closer, drawn in by the tiny houses, steepled church, and an adorable skating rink.

"You even have cute little skaters."

"Watch this." He pressed a button and the skaters did a mini-circuit of the village rink.

Love! "And look at these two." A couple of figures held hands while looking over the bridge back toward the cozy, glow-lit village. She was instantly jealous.

Of the inanimate objects.

"My family sends me new pieces every year to add to it. I know it's kind of silly but it looks like my hometown of Ö-vik, or how it looked in the last century." He sounded a little shy.

"I think it's great that you have these holiday traditions."

"Don't you have some in your family?"

"Not really." A sudden urge to reveal something more personal gripped her. "I'm an only child and to be honest, my parents are kind of self-involved. They weren't neglectful or anything, just not terribly interested in shaping a little human."

His gaze seared her. "So you're a self-made woman."

"That makes it sound like I've achieved something."

"Haven't you? You've got a good job, a cat, friends. I'm sure Harper can't manage without you."

When he put it like that, it didn't sound so bad. Andrew had considered her unambitious and lacking in drive. Truth was, she liked the jobs she'd had since college. Keeping people organized and helping them perform at their peak was an undervalued commodity. From the outside—or her ex's version of it—her life might look dull and uninspired, but she was fulfilled.

It was her personal life that kept coming up short.

She took another glance around. "You live alone?"

He tilted his head, amused. "Perhaps you think it's strange for a grown man who gets struck by pucks for a living to enjoy the holidays so much?"

She grinned. "Oh, I'm not judging. I love Christmas as well." Or she used to. She hadn't bothered to put up any decorations or a tree this year. "I've just never met anyone who would go to all this trouble without anyone to ..." *Share it.* That's what she'd been about to say, like the big foot-in-mouth clod she was.

"We celebrate Yule in a big way back in Sweden. The season lasts a while there but I usually can't go home for it. So I bring it here instead."

"Don't your family come to visit?"

"They have in the past. My parents were here a few weeks ago but they didn't want to spend Christmas here because my sister is about to have a baby any day now."

When she first met him seven years ago, he had talked about his homesickness. To listen to him, he still had pangs of it—of course, that was to be expected at this time of year for family who were close. A time for togetherness.

She didn't know what that was like. The yearning she understood, but her own family weren't all that interested in connecting like that.

"Last year I had some of the single guys over and I cooked," Erik said. "This year, it's just me but I still somehow managed to make the same amount of food."

"So that's what that smell is ... it's delicious."

He was delicious. Even in that funny apron, there was no distracting from his powerful build. With broad shoulders accented by the tiny straps, he had retied the strings so it cinched slightly and highlighted his trim hips. Underneath, he wore a navy-blue Henley, a snug fit against his biceps and rolled up to reveal a smattering of fair hair on his forearms. The forearms led to his hands—as forearms usually did—and now her mind was flooded with images of those hands as they held her fast so he could lick inside her.

Forget seven seconds in Heaven. More like seven minutes ... and every one of them was imprinted on her lizard brain. Now she ogled him like he was as appetizing as whatever dish he was cooking up.

Full circle back to the food. Nicely done.

"I could probably help you eat some of it. Just to be a good guest."

"That's kind of you." He stepped closer and her pulse started to hammer. She always got like this around him, even when watching him on TV. They had a history. Up until last night, a *secret* history, one that she alternately cursed and treasured. Now she was here and they had done wicked, wonderful things together. It was a heady elixir.

Keanu made a sound like a dog.

Erik frowned. "Is he okay?"

"Define okay." At his eyebrow quirk, she elaborated. "He's fine. I just need to set up his food, maybe in ..." She looked around. Usually she stashed his bowl in the kitchen but if Erik was cooking, she didn't want to get in his way. "You're sure you want a stinky cat litter box in your home?"

"Have you spent much time in a pro-hockey locker room, Casey? Or eaten pickled herring in multiple preparations? I'm used to funk, cat or otherwise. And I grew up with animals."

She didn't want anything to overshadow what was happening. If Keanu ruined this for her ...

Ruined what? It was just lunch.

"Perhaps the office?" he asked. "Let me show you."

The office was actually Erik's trophy room. It contained framed pictures of the team and nice cherry wood furniture. An IKEA joke was on the tip of her tongue, but no doubt he'd heard that more than once. Against one wall stood a display case celebrating the man's significant accomplishments. She knew his bio inside out and it was fun to see his awards and hardware up close.

"Oh, your Vezina!" That was for the NHL's best goaltender. "And the Viking award." Voted on by other Swedish players in the NHL, this had always struck her as one of the more fun ones. Erik was the only goalie to have ever received it. "I love that your countrymen decide this."

"It's special for sure."

A media cabinet held a number of DVDs, mostly hockey, and other sports like soccer and curling, which she had never understood.

"You have the entire series of *The Office* on Blu-ray."

"I know you can stream all the episodes now, but when I first started watching it, DVDs were the way to go. I don't know if you remembered but we talked about *The Office* that night in the bar. I had never seen it. I bought this and watched all of them. The boxset has the webisodes, commentaries, and blooper reels."

He had watched it because she recommended it. Her heart fluttered wildly.

"This room is far too nice for my cat's, uh ..."

"Throne of shit?"

She laughed. "One way to describe it."

"There is a utility room but it's one level down and a bit of a trek for your kitty. Don't worry about it. It's good to be reminded that with the glory there is also the cat poop. Keeps me grounded." He winked at her, then wedged the door open so Keanu could come and go freely. Casey set up his litter box, water and food, hiding his medication in it though her cat gave a knowing look. It was the game.

"I can't guarantee he won't scratch your furniture." In another lifetime she might have been worried about the Christmas trees but the lowest branches were too high to tempt him. At this elderly stage, he wouldn't be jumping to grab anything shiny.

"I had cats growing up. The little assholes will do what they're going to do. We can only accept our fates." He placed a hand at her back. "Let me get you something to drink."

Loving the intimacy of that large hand touching her lightly, she let him guide her to an amazing kitchen with the counters laden with dishes—meat, vegetables, some cold, some warming on the stove. The air was fragrant with the scent of roasting.

"Wine, beer, schnapps?"

"White wine, if you have it."

While he poured she looked around. "This is a fabulous space."

"I like to cook."

"Were you really going to eat all this by yourself?"

He shrugged one broad shoulder, then handed off a glass of wine. "I'll be talking to my family later on FaceTime and they'll wonder what I did. They like to see I'm getting into the spirit of Julafton. Christmas is important to them."

And to the man before her. Again, her heart keened for him.

"You must miss them, especially at this time of year."

"I do. Are you close with your family?"

"Not terribly. My parents are lovely people but they've always treated me as a grown-up, even when I wasn't." Not the most indulgent of parental units, they had spent her childhood indulging in their love for each other. She had always felt in the way. "It's not a bad thing, but it means they don't really fuss over me. Which is fine, really!"

She sounded pitiful. How could she miss something she had never had? Independent from a young age, she had refused to rely on anyone until Andrew. Yet talking about her parents made her feel like she wasn't enough for them.

For anyone.

When Erik remained quiet, she rushed to fill the lull. "They're on a cruise. In the Caribbean."

"Their loss is my gain."

"You just needed someone to help you get through this." Suddenly self-conscious about her situation comparing so poorly to Erik's familial perfection, she turned to the first dish she saw, a plate of cocktail sausages. "What's this?"

Sausages, dummy.

"That's prinskorv. Also known as Prince Sausages."

"And this?"

"Rödkål. Cabbage and apple salad."

He had moved closer and her pulse spiked in anticipation. But first, she needed to do something. Take some measure of control.

"Erik, we should clear the air."

"Should we?"

She nodded, took a sip of her wine. "I've been mad at you for a while now and it wasn't fair."

"It was fair. It was very fair. But I hope I made up for it" —he winked, the sexy Swedish rogue—"and if I didn't, I will continue to try."

"You don't have to—"

"With my cooking."

"Oh." Did she sound disappointed that only food was on the menu? "I'm sure you'll be completely forgiven as soon as I eat some sausage."

His lips twitched.

"I meant this sausage!" She pointed at the dish.

Full-on smirk now.

"Oh, shut up!" She laughed and he joined in, the first

time she'd heard him laugh in years. Sometimes he chuckled in interviews or in the office with Harper, but not since that night in the Empty Net had she heard him laugh because of something she said. People said laughter was the best medicine, but there was more to it. Making someone happy was a self-soothing heart balm in itself.

"Casey, I don't want to make you uncomfortable. This is just lunch—there's no expectation." He leaned against the counter. "Yet you seem upset."

"I do?"

"Yes, you get this funny little wrinkle around your mouth when you are unhappy. I've seen it at least eight times over the last year."

Whenever she glared at him in the reception area outside Harper's office. He had been watching her all this time, gauging her mood. Equally, she had been hyperaware of him. Every moment he spent in the office her body had existed in a tug of war between desire and disdain.

Right now, desire was doing a victory lap.

"I'm having mixed feelings about the no expectation thing."

"You are?"

"Maybe I'd like some expectations." It shouldn't all be up to him. Why couldn't she take the initiative? She set her glass on the counter, placed a hand on his chest, and pressed, just to get a sense of what she was dealing with. Oh my. In the intervening years, he'd become even more rock solid.

"I need to kiss you," she whispered. More a ragged sound.

"Not as much as I need to ki—"

Their mouths met and it was white-hot and crazy, a product of deep and powerful need. His hands cupped her ass and kneaded, bringing her close to his hard body. The kiss went on, a blaze of want distilled to mouths and tongues. She tangled her hands in his hair, loving how it felt to get right in there in an eminently physical way.

A wail went up from the other room.

He drew back, his eyes dark and smoky with lust. "Someone needs attention," she muttered. *Her. She needed all his attention.*

"We should eat. And talk."

That night in the bar she had loved talking to him. They had clicked—or so she thought. She yearned for that again.

"Okay, let's eat and talk."

9

"Just a little bit more, Casey. You barely touched my sausage."

"I had three servings!" She gazed at the table; it looked like they'd hardly made a dent in the julbord, a Christmas smorgasbord of such variety it was hard to believe one man had created it all.

Before they ate, Erik took photos to send to his family—apparently this was key to ensuring they wouldn't worry about him—and then he made her try everything. Each bite had been amazing, though she drew the line at pickled herring (Keanu had no such scruples.) They hadn't even got to the sweets yet, another impressive collection of cookies and marzipan-covered treats that she couldn't wait to try once some room was cleared in her stomach.

He poured a shot of something clear, and clearly alcoholic, into a couple of small glasses.

"What's this?" She lifted it to her nostrils and let them be tickled by its pungent herbal scent.

"Swedish schnapps, also known as aquavit. It's more of a

midsummer thing, but when the guys are over during the holidays, I like to indulge them."

"You play up your Swedishness for the crowd?"

"Something like that." His eyes sparkled. "But before you drink, we have to sing."

"Sing?"

He nodded. "Yes, we sing a snapsvisa. A drinking song."

"Okay, you first."

That made him laugh, a deep-chested sound that went right to her core. "Alright, let me see." He placed a hand over his heart and launched into an upbeat ditty, in Swedish, of course, and while she had no clue what it meant, she had never been so entranced. His voice was strong and sonorous and sent a thrill through her blood.

"Skål!" Erik lifted his glass and knocked it back.

"What does that mean?"

"Skål? To your health."

"No, the song."

He poured another shot. "It is called 'Hej, tomtegubbar' and is a song to Santa, about how life is short and we should fill our glasses and be jolly. We have songs about frogs, bees, vodka on a string, the Finns. Several about the Finns. One of my favorites is about teaching your mother-in-law to swim but then losing her beneath the waves when you take a moment to drink your schnapps."

"That's kind of dark."

"The winters are long, Casey, and our entertainments sometimes take a turn for the macabre." He flashed that goofy grin, sending her heart into a tailspin. "Now, your turn."

Oh, dear. "I don't know any."

"Of course you do. There must be some folk songs in your culture."

Her culture was bland and boring compared to Erik's. Folk songs, folk songs ... A notion struck her.

"So it might take me a second to remember the words." She took a breath and started, fumbling for the lyrics from a deep, dark recess in her brain.

"Making your way ... in the world today takes everything you've got ..."

Watching Erik's bright eyes, she waited for that glimmer of recognition. Of course, her off-tune rendition could mean he might never get it. Or maybe he had never heard it.

By the time she got to the last line, "Where everybody knows your name," he was nodding along but clearly not realizing she had ripped off a TV theme song. So her culture was an ode to sit-coms and the *Cheers* theme was the best of the bunch.

"That was amazing!" He handed her the glass. "Now drink."

A light sip left her in no doubt of the powerful alcohol content, like vodka but with flavor. Better to go all in. "Skål!" She downed it and coughed. "Wow! That's strong stuff."

"You didn't have to drink it in one go." But his tone said he appreciated her being a sport.

"When in Sweden."

He smiled and there went another one of the ice bricks walling her heart.

"How is Keanu, I wonder?" All through lunch, Erik had been as hospitable to her cat as he was to her, always checking in to make sure he was doing okay.

Keanu was currently lying before the fire, staring at the tree with malevolent intent. "He liked the herring. It's not often he gets such a stinky fishy treat."

"Well, he has been very brave in this new place. So have you."

"I have?"

He circled the lip of his glass with his index finger. "You didn't have to come over. You could have tortured me all through the holidays. Really committed to your revenge."

She didn't want to be that person. And she didn't want him thinking she was that person.

"I was angry but it's silly to be so annoyed. It was just a night where two people hooked up. I shouldn't have made it out to be more than it was. I can't expect you to remember all these years later."

"But I did remember."

"Just not my face. And I get it, it's fine! I had different hair and a different name and it was dark and we were drinking. There are plenty of reasons why I wouldn't stand out."

He shook his head, his eyebrows slammed together. "Please don't think you didn't make an impression. You did. I never forgot you. I tried to find you but—" He broke off, gusting out a breath. This situation was still bothering him, much more so than it should. She wanted them both to move on, yet her fragile ego also wanted to hear more about him trying to find her.

"But?"

"Perhaps if I had more schnapps, it would be easier to tell you."

She placed her hand over his. "You can tell me anything, Erik. I know I was awful before but I promise I won't be the Judgy McJudge-face of the past. You're looking at a new nonjudgmental, uh, McJudge-face." She giggled, the aquavit, along with the bottle of wine they'd shared over lunch buzzing a path through her veins. "Tell me."

He squeezed her hand and turned it over, tracing a finger along the lifeline on her palm. "It's going to sound strange and you might not believe me but hear me out. I have a condition."

"Okay."

"It's called face blindness."

She blinked, confused. "Face ... blindness?"

"Well, it has a more complicated medical name but that's essentially what it is. I have a hard time recognizing faces. I usually have to use cues like hair and face shape and clothing. It's not personal to you or to anyone. I see you in front of me now. I recognize that you are Casey and that you are the most beautiful woman I've ever seen, yet when I saw the most beautiful woman I had ever seen *again*, I didn't recognize her."

Surely he was joking. This was that dark Swedish humor, borne of a culture that had drinking songs about drowning a mother-in-law.

But one look at his face made it clear: this was no joke.

"This is a real thing, isn't it?"

He nodded.

"Tell me about it."

"Some people get it after an injury. Other people are born with it. I had an uncle with it, so it's genetic for me. I've had it all my life but you come up with ways to compensate. Fake your way through interactions with people you don't know well. Even with people you do know."

Shock rolled through her, quickly chased by guilt. She didn't completely understand what had happened but she knew this much: this mess was all her fault.

"Erik, I can't believe I was so harsh on you. I thought you were just another inconsiderate jock who wham-banged without a thought to anyone's feelings. And now you're telling me—" She covered her mouth, the enormity of how she had treated him coming on full force.

The man had a medical condition!

"Casey, it's okay. You didn't know. And I had no idea that was the problem between us. If I'd known it was because I didn't recognize you, because what's wrong with *me* hurt you, I would have done something about it sooner."

She shook her head. "What's wrong with *you*? There's nothing wrong with you! I should have come clean instead of acting like a spurned lover."

She stood, feeling unsteady and incredibly foolish. She had been so awful to him and now she wasn't sure she could ever make it up to him.

"Casey ..."

"I'll be back in a sec—" The last syllable was smothered by a sob as she ran to the bathroom.

WHAT THE HELL JUST HAPPENED?

Erik shouldn't have said anything. He merely wanted her to know that he could never forget her, not really. That it was his fault they were in this weird situation. She needn't feel any guilt about this whatsoever.

"Any words of advice, Keanu?"

Taking on the mantle of his owner's disapproval, the cat refused to give him the time of day.

"I agree. It's a tough one."

After waiting a couple of minutes with no sign of Casey, he knocked on the bathroom door. "Are you okay?"

"Yeah-yes, I'm fine. Go back to lunch. I'll just be a second."

He waited a few seconds, then placed his ear to the door. Sniffling sounds came through.

"Are you crying?"

"No, not at all." It definitely sounded teary.

"Could you open the door, please?"

"Just a moment."

"Now, Casey."

Two seconds later, the door was unlocked but remained closed. He took it as an invitation and turned the knob.

She stood by the sink, tissue in hand, eyes watery and red-rimmed.

"I'm fine. Really. I'm—"

He took her in his arms and wrapped her up like a gift. A few seconds ticked by while he let himself enjoy this—not her despair, just holding her close. She felt so, so good against him.

She peeked up at him. "Happy holidays?"

He chuckled. "This is how you usually celebrate?"

"Oh, yeah. Great food and drinking songs, followed by a meltdown that maneuvers me into the embrace of a hot hockey hunk."

"We'll have to call around and see if we can find one for you."

She leaned her forehead on his chest. "I'm such a mess. I'm sorry."

"You know, you're going to have to stop apologizing. Perhaps we can both stop and just move on. I screwed up. You screwed up. But now we're here and it's …"

"It's …"

"Better than I could have dreamed."

She peered at him. Sniffed again. "Who are you?"

"Just Erik Jorgenson, goaltender for the Chicago Rebels, sometimes not the most thoughtful of people but my heart is in the right place, I think. I like you, Casey. I liked you when you were Coco and I liked you when you didn't like me and I like you when you're happy and when you're sad."

"What about when I'm ... in the mood?"

Oh, he especially liked her then. But he wouldn't take advantage. She was feeling raw after what he had told her, maybe even ... grateful.

"In the mood for dessert? Sure."

She kissed him, the sweetest treat he could have imagined. And he could imagine a lot.

He didn't mean to moan or curl his tongue around hers or grab her perfect ass, but all those things happened. Her fingers tunneled through his hair as she held him fast to her lips. In two seconds, he had her on the vanity, his body rocking and rolling between her thighs. He was desperate for her, panting for relief.

He yanked back and held her firm with his hands on her hips.

"What's wrong?"

Looking at her kiss-stung lips, lust-stoked pupils, and high color, only one response came to mind: *nothing. This is perfect. You are perfect.*

But his dick was not the boss of him. "We need to slow down."

"We do?"

"Casey, I just told you something about me, something that I don't tell just anyone. And you got upset because you felt you had done me wrong. You didn't, but I saw how you reacted and now you might want to ... make up for that somehow." He rubbed a hand over his painful erection, the one he had been sporting since he ran into her at Rebels HQ last night. "I want nothing more than to bury my cock inside you, feel you tight around me, bring you off until you scream—"

"Then, do it."

"Not while you're upset. Not until you're sure you don't feel you have to apologize with your beautiful body."

"I don't. I mean, I don't feel like that."

He shrugged, though it actually hurt his dick to do so. "I need to put the food away and tidy up. Maybe you could choose something to watch on Netflix?"

"Netflix and chill, Erik?" She gave him a wicked grin. "Knew we'd get there."

"Get your mind out of the gutter, Casey Higgins." He moved closer and rubbed his thumbs under her eyes. "Are you still upset?"

"Yes, but for a completely different reason," she grumbled.

He kissed her nose, then her cheekbones, then each closed eye before finishing with a light press to her lips. Anything more and he might not be responsible for his actions.

"What's that sound?" she murmured.

My heart fighting to get out of my chest. Just the usual around you.

"I think it's your phone?"

She was right. "Come on, I want you to meet someone."

10

Erik picked up his phone and hit the accept button for the call. With his other hand, he held hers tight. Like so much with Erik, it was adorable.

"Mamma!" Followed by a string of fast-talking Swedish. He sat on the sofa, bringing Casey with him. She tried to stay out of the camera's range, but he was having none of it.

"This is Casey, Mamma. She came over for Julafton."

A blond woman with Erik's eyes smiled back from the screen. "Oh, hello! It's so nice to meet you."

"It's lovely to meet you, as well. I'm sorry I don't know how to say Merry—oh, wait a second, I do. God Jul!" It came out sounding like Keanu had coughed up a hairball.

Erik's grin added even more brightness to the festive surroundings and her heart skipped, knowing she had produced that sun. "You remembered?"

"It was only this morning."

"Yes, but—"

"Erik!" Mama Jorgenson had been replaced by a trio of blonde beauties staring out from the screen. They all screamed in unison, then launched into more breathlessly-paced Swedish. Erik said *ya* and *uh huh* every few seconds, but it didn't make much difference to the torrent of speech.

Erik finally got a word in. "Casey, these are my very rude sisters: Elsa, Julia, and Astrid. You can just treat them as the same person, which is what I do. Growing up I could only tell the difference between them because they were a few inches apart in height. Then they all caught up to the oldest, Elsa, so now it doesn't matter which is which."

He smiled, obviously seeing the humor in it, though it had to be difficult.

"Erik, stop being so pitiful," one of his sisters said in English, probably out of politeness to include Casey. "You know who I am!"

"Yes, you're the most annoying one. I can tell by the strange frequency in your voice, only recognizable by brothers and dogs."

This produced another rush of talking, eventually interrupted by a deep, male voice. A genial-looking man took over the phone.

"God Jul, min son!"

"God Jul, Pappa. Meet Casey, my guest for Julafton."

"Hello, Casey, I hope my son has fed you well."

She smiled. "Very well. He's extremely talented in the kitchen."

"Ya, he will have this to fall back on when hockey is ended."

Erik grinned at her. "My father is realistic. He thinks I'm lucky to have lasted this long in the NHL."

"Not lucky. You are a hard worker. We miss you."

"I miss you, too, Pappa."

"Do you miss me?" One of the sister's voices rang through, then a different supermodel came on, followed by a troop of children—likely nieces and nephews—every one of them happy to switch to perfect English once they realized that Erik had a non-Swedish-speaking guest.

"It's time for gifts!" Someone screeched, and then the next ten minutes were spent opening packages that Erik must have sent home.

His mother chimed in. "We must hope that Erik can make up for our rudeness as we don't have any gifts for Casey."

"Oh, no, please don't worry about that! I love seeing all of you going to town on the wrapping paper."

"I'll open mine later, except for this one." Erik held up a small box. "I think I know what it is." He opened it and pulled out a small wooden horse. Casey had seen these before—Dala horses were a traditional Swedish symbol. This one was red with exquisitely-painted decorative art.

He hopped up and, still keeping the phone's camera lens in position, he placed the ornament on the tree. He said a few words in Swedish, low and almost prayerful.

Returning to the sofa, he sat and squeezed her hand again. Her heart flipped over again, as she felt privileged to be part of this experience with him. Obviously this gift exchange was incredibly meaningful.

One of the sisters cut through the moment with more Swedish. They seemed to be looking more closely at her now, then one of them said something that sounded like "Coco."

Casey glanced at Erik, who looked a bit squirrely. *Coco?*

Erik muttered something—gah, more Swedish!—which set everyone off into amazed chatter. Thirty seconds later, he ended the call.

"One of your sisters said Coco. Was that about me?"

"I may have texted Elsa earlier about you coming over

for lunch and I may have mentioned our history. She knows I was excited to have you over."

"Why were you excited? I've been nothing but horrid to you."

"Horrid? That's a very Harry Potter word. And a little over the top."

"Erik, I was all wrong about you."

"Don't know about that. I didn't make it easy for you." He curled a finger around one of her springy locks. "But then I wonder if you even make it easy on yourself."

"Why do you say that?"

"Because you seem to be taking the news hard. Forgive yourself, Casey."

It was a strange thing to say but also completely on the nose. For the last year, she had been berating herself for being such a pushover with Andrew, to the point that she had gone to the other end of the spectrum. Trust was in short supply, forgiveness even more so. Perhaps that's what needed to happen: not just trust of Erik but trusting her own instincts.

She wanted to kiss him again. Badly. But she didn't want what had happened before to happen again. To be pushed away.

Instead she said, "Let's tidy up."

Casey took a closer look at Tomte sitting on the mantel above the fireplace. She lifted Keanu up to meet him.

"This is your new friend, Keanu."

"Tomte is friend to no one," Erik said behind her.

She turned, and Keanu took the opportunity to spring from her hands and leave the room in a feline huff.

"Why not?"

"He's known for being overly sensitive and prone to revenge if he's disrespected."

"My kind of elf."

His expression said she was unwise to mock. "If I don't put out risgrynsgröt for him tonight—that's Christmas porridge—he will probably kill me in my sleep. Or maim me for fun."

"These are your Christmas traditions?"

He tilted his head. She was starting to develop a thing for that head tilt. "We are somewhat morbid in Sweden."

"Well, you wouldn't know it to listen to your family who are adorable. When will you see them next?"

"I go home in the summertime. It's always good to see everyone. I've been here for seven years and it feels like …" He shook his head.

"It feels like what?"

"Like they are all moving on with their lives, carving a place for themselves. Each year, there are new additions to the family. New kids, new pets, new boyfriends. They sometimes find a spare minute to come visit me. But that's the way it is as we get older—everyone has their own lives, moves on to new things. Even the team, all of them meeting their one true person."

His melancholy resonated with the weight in her chest. "You haven't fallen for anyone all this time you've been here?" As far as she and her Google alert on him knew, he'd never been pictured with anyone but that probably meant he was good at keeping his sex life under the radar.

Or maybe he just forgot everyone he ever took to bed.

His look was so intense she shivered. For a moment, she worried he might not have heard her. Finally, he answered, "There have been some women that I've been interested in, but they're usually interested in someone else. I don't have the best luck. Not the kind of guy girls go for, I suppose."

The man was six feet and change of rock solid Viking stock, or maybe that was Norwegian. Either way, there was no missing him. "I went for you."

He was practically on top of her now, yet not touching. So close, yet miles away from where she needed him.

"That night, all those years ago, you said you had just ended a relationship. You were looking for some fun, with no consequences. Yet, I wanted there to be consequences. I wanted there to be more than fun."

Her heart caught. Erik had a way of speaking straight to the crux of the matter.

"I felt like we had a moment then," he continued. "A connection that was more than just alcohol and lust. And when I didn't see you again, when you didn't seek me out, I assumed that was just me."

Oh God, this was awful. All the things he said were true: she'd wanted a night of no-strings fun, had wanted to lose herself in the moment. Yet she *had* felt a pull to him, so much so that it hurt like hell when he didn't call her.

"It was a strange night. A strange time. I'd just broken up with Andrew, my boyfriend of a year. He said he wasn't ready for anything long-term. When you didn't call, I wasn't going to take the initiative. You had the advantage of being famous and I assumed you wouldn't want your non-famous one-night stand turning up. A month later, Andrew was back and we were a couple again."

She had fallen back into her rut, any ghost of a chance with the man who rocked her world a distant memory. She should have listened to the voice telling her that getting back with Andrew was a mistake. Seven years wasted.

"Where is this boyfriend now?"

"Probably in an eggnog-induced coma, lying on top of his new girlfriend, the younger, hotter model."

Swedish eyebrow raise, which seemed more sardonic than an American one.

"We broke up again for the last time just before I started working at the Rebels," she explained. "It's why I was so sensitive when you and I met again a year ago. About ... everything." She had become so prickly, so suspicious of men, and look what happened. She let it color everything and didn't give Erik the benefit of the doubt.

"And why you were so anxious to get your revenge in that closet last night." He moved closer, his lips a mere heartbeat away. "Twice."

"That wasn't me. I mean, it wasn't *like* me. I'm not usually so demanding."

"It was hot as fuck."

"Yeah?"

"Oh, yeah." He kissed her.

And immediately stopped.

"Sorry, I should have—"

She didn't let him finish, or rather she finished for him, taking what she needed. More of Erik's lips, taste, essence. No more second-guessing. No more overthinking. She had met his family, for God's sake!

That made her giggle.

"What?"

"I'm just—ignore me, Erik. I'm kind of losing my mind here."

"In a good way?" His breath fanned her lips, his eyes dark with longing.

"In the best way. I need this right now. I need you."

He stood back and peeled off his shirt, a move that left her gaping. Because ... muscles.

She had seen them before, years ago.

She had seen them more recently in the Rebels holiday calendar—she might have spent a little more time than was healthy drooling over Mr. December—and the couple of times she had walked into the locker room to deliver a message.

But in the flesh and now, it was different. Muscles on muscles, not an ounce of fat, and this man could eat. Where did he put it?

"You're absolutely ... unreal." She reached for his pec and let her fingertips wander. His eyes flickered shut for a moment, then opened and felled her with all that blue.

"Lie down, Casey."

"Here?" There was a rug and a fire and they were in a winter wonderland, so maybe ...

"I'll just be a second."

He left the room while she considered if this was a good idea. What would happen after?

Probably nothing, which would be fine.

This was just scratching an itch. Maybe even repaying a favor. He had been very generous in that closet.

He returned with pillows and a comforter and laid them down on the rug.

"You are still upright." He smiled, a rakish grin. "Let's change that."

11

Erik was nervous.

He shouldn't be. He had been here before, last night and all those years ago. But this was different. Make or break. If he fucked up—and God knew if anyone could fuck this up it would be him—he wouldn't get another shot.

So he was nervous.

Only so was she.

"We don't have to do this," he said. *Please say you want to do this.*

"You keep doing that," she said, biting her lip. "Being such a gentleman. Giving me an out at every opportunity."

"I want to be clear. Last time—seven years ago—there was a lot of alcohol involved. And last night, I sort of backed you into a corner—"

"And made me come. Twice."

"Right." His smile felt painted on. "But it didn't seem real. It seemed like a moment from some fantasy. A dark closet, a holiday party, an apology that was a long time coming. Now ... now, I want to get it right." Build on the foundations of their truce.

She pulled her fluffy white sweater over her head, dropped it on an armchair, and sat down on the rug. The sweater move left her hair adorably static-y but he didn't dwell on that too long because …

Breasts. Gorgeous fucking tits wrapped in a sexy cream bra. The view from above was spectacular.

He suspected it would be even better when he was lying down.

"Everything you've done since you found out who I was has been right, Erik. Even before that. Nothing you do could be wrong. You're a really good guy."

He fell to his knees, a move he was familiar with on the ice where he had to defend his goal. Now he was in a crouch, wondering if he would have to defend his heart from this woman. If he'd already let her sneak in too far.

Her eyes were soft, imploring. She had been hurt, not just by him but by this jerk she had spent all those years with. Someone who couldn't appreciate her.

Appreciation began tonight.

"Lie down, Casey." He positioned the pillow at one end of the rug and guided her to it, so she was spread out before the fire like a Julafton feast. Where to start?

With a kiss, of course, between those gorgeous tits. He applied his lips to the dip there and added a lick that made her shiver.

"I have to apologize in advance."

"For what?" She sounded a little breathless.

"For taking my time. This will be frustrating for you."

She smirked. "You think? We'll see how long you last, Jorgenson."

Quite a while as it happened. About ten minutes later, she was down to her underwear and he had found ticklish areas, pleasure points, sensitive patches of skin that told him more about this woman than any words could.

"Erik," she panted. "How are you doing?"

He looked up from where he had been spending the last three minutes—the soft round of her belly—and met her gaze.

"How am *I* doing?"

"Y-yes. Aren't you a little anxious to get on with it?"

A light brush of his lips across her abdomen drew her shiver. "Perhaps I should tell you what I did last night after you abandoned me in that closet at Chase Manor."

She inhaled a jagged breath.

"I came home and took a cold shower." He moved his lips over the front of her panties. They had cat's whiskers on them. "Then I started cooking. I needed to because—well, I needed to prepare for Julafton but it also helped." He kissed the soft fabric, enjoying the springy softness of her mound and the scent of her arousal. "Helped me resist certain urges."

"Erik, are you saying that—you—uh—didn't take care of business last night?" She sat up. "Guess it wasn't that exciting for you!"

He cupped her jaw and drew her lips to his. "I held back from jerking off because I wanted this. You. Today. It was your sweet wet pussy that drove me mad, now I want to be inside you when I come."

For a moment, he worried his dirty talk would put her off, but she gave a full body shiver that felt like pleasure. "No need to wait any longer."

"Is that impatience I hear?"

"Maybe a little. A lot. Just—" Her eyes rolled back in her head as he rubbed the front of her panties, over the growing dampness. "*Please.*"

A moan-prayer-demand that ratcheted his dick into painful territory and his heart into triple time.

No more delays. He rolled her underwear off and separated her thighs so he could form his plan of attack.

"Wh-what are you doing?"

"Getting a proper look. Seven years ago, I was half-drunk. Last night, I was half-blind. Now, there is no escaping my gaze. I want to see every pulse of this pretty pussy, how wet my touch makes you, the velvet that will soon be wrapped around my cock and milking me good. I don't want to miss a thing."

With both of his hands on her thighs he coasted his fingertips up over the soft flesh until his thumbs reached her slick folds. One testing stroke sent her into a full shudder, her back arching, her body straining for more.

"Good?"

Her smile was a blessing. "Fishing for compliments, Fish?"

"Maybe." He parted her with his fingers, then used those same fingers to hook inside her and rub.

"That's—oh, that's so good."

But it could be better. He stroked through all that pink, circling her clit, figuring out how much pressure produced the best response. Her pleasure was his mission and right now, every touch was mission-critical.

Within seconds, she was writhing against his fingertips, a slave to the sensations shivering through her. With one last stroke, she came and nothing had ever turned him on more.

He would give her a moment to relax. Or at least that was his plan, but she wasn't having any of it.

"Condom. Now."

He handed it to her, and while she ripped it open, he stripped to total nakedness.

She gasped. "The gods were having a good day when they made you, Erik."

Protection secured, she dug her fingers into his biceps, pulling him over her. "I want to feel the weight of you," she whispered. "Your solidity. I want to be in no doubt that you're here and that this isn't a dream."

He wasn't sure he understood that, but if she meant that she needed an anchor, he could be that for her. If she needed a weight to hold on to during a choppy time in her life, he could be that. Or perhaps she needed to be well-fucked. He could do that as well.

He grasped her hand, interlocking their fingers, realizing he needed something to hold on to as well. And as he slid into her in one smooth, hot stroke, he never dropped his gaze from hers. Committing his body—and more—completely.

CASEY WAS LIVING some sort of holiday-induced fever dream. Her fantasy was inside her, his solidity the only thing keeping her tethered to this reality. His eyes consumed her, and she remembered how they had stripped her bare that first time. Exposed her completely. Only now, she wondered if she would survive all the messy emotions pinballing around her chest.

No one expected anything from a one-night stand (Casey did once, but she grew out of that nonsense real quick). She shouldn't expect anything here, but would she be able to fake any semblance of casual?

She wanted him so much.

So she would do her level best to limit it to the physical, the sensation, the orgasms.

"You feel so good," she whispered in his ear. "Like you're meant to be here."

She meant inside her, but she might have meant more. Maybe she'd be better off zipping her lips because talking would only get her into trouble. There was something oddly fated about this moment, the weight of it.

The weight of him.

He withdrew, plunged again. The depth of his reach astonished her. He grasped her ass in his giant palm and gave a filthy, possessive squeeze.

"This is perfect." Another squeeze, his breath labored, his words strained. "You are perfect."

She wanted to believe him. She ached everywhere. Her breasts, her pussy, every extremity in a throb of want and desire.

"More. Please, Erik."

His next thrust pushed her a few inches up, creating a friction with the rug that she knew she would feel tomorrow. She didn't want to think of the sensual evidence he was leaving on her body or the tracks he was trailing over her heart.

Each new thrust found another point of light.

"Casey, Casey," he murmured against her lips before pausing his strokes to consume her with a kiss. His grip on her butt cheek was unyielding as he fucked her so hard she saw stars.

There were a million things to love about being here with Erik. His absolute commitment to her enjoyment. The way his body strained, muscles bunching and hands controlling, as he moved fluidly inside her. The innately physical sensation of desire and pleasure, that should feel familiar, yet felt brand new.

But mostly she got off on his blue-eyed intensity, how Erik's heart and soul was reflected in his burning gaze. And when she came again and he followed her over, she knew that was what would stay with her.

SHE LAY in his arms under the comforter, her hand tracing circles on his chest. The most impressive chest she'd ever seen, to be honest. The fire's intensity had ebbed, shadowing the sexy shenanigans on the hearth, but the embers still glowed.

"So, what's it like?"

"What?"

"The face thing."

His eyebrows had drawn together but quickly relaxed. Erik wasn't one for dwelling on the bad stuff. She loved that about him.

"When I was younger, I just thought I was stupid. I would run into people at parties, even family parties, and my brain seemed to lock up. I found myself waiting for clues, usually a voice or a manner of speaking. Or I would try to focus on a person's hair, try to remember how it was parted or where it fell over their ears. I didn't even realize I was doing it until I was older, after I had developed coping mechanisms. Then one day someone told a story about how my uncle had picked up the wrong little girl from school."

"Oh, wow."

He nodded. "Right. He figured it out quickly and apologized but then he came clean and said that he had been diagnosed with prosopagnosia. That's the official name for it. I did all the research I could, and told my father that I might have it, too. It can be mild or severe. Mine is on the milder end. Some people with more serious conditions don't even recognize their own faces in the mirror."

"That's awful!"

"Yes, it is. I'm lucky in that I know my own face. I see it on the Jumbotron when the players are introduced and I'm fairly certain that's me. I am the only player with this perfect flow, you know."

She chuckled, enjoying this side of him. Though he wasn't wrong. The man had wicked flow.

"But sometimes in the locker room or the player lounge, I have to wait for someone to speak. There are a lot of tall, dark-haired guys—"

"Dreamy."

He pinched her butt lightly. "No lusting after my teammates!"

She laughed. "Sorry, you describe them so well. But it's abstract. None of them really appeal—I like 'em blond and blue-eyed with many muscles, amazing flow, wicked cooking skills, and deep voices that sing strange songs about frogs and Finns."

That made him chuckle. "I will make sure none of that changes if it's what you like, Casey."

The way he said her name, the way he held her gaze, was like being drugged. High on Erik.

"So you sometimes can't tell the difference between …" She thought about it. "Kershaw and Durand, for example?" He was right. A lot of them were tall, dark, and handsome. Somewhat indistinguishable if you only had body type to go on.

"Theo has more interesting hair. He spends a lot of time on it and when he speaks, there's no confusion. Such a drama queen. Reid often looks annoyed, which I can figure out, probably because he was on that sex fast for so long."

"Not anymore from what I've heard."

He smiled. "Living with an attractive woman while you are restricting your diet in all things is probably not the easiest or smartest thing to do. He is very much in love with Kennedy but she is leaving."

Casey wasn't so sure. Of Reid's love for his roommate-slash-dog nanny, yes. But Kennedy might be willing to stick around if the cranky Canadian could only get his head out of his ass.

"I think those crazy kids will work it out," she said.

"What about us crazy kids? Will we work it out?"

"What do you think *this* is?" She ran a hand over his chest and down to his stomach. "If not working something out?"

"Sexual frustration, you mean? I think we should date."

"Erik—"

"Hear me out, Casey. If I knew who you were a year ago when we met again, I would have asked you out. Immediately."

"And I would have said no."

He blinked. "Really?"

"I'd just exited a long relationship. I was feeling pretty raw and trying to be good at my job, which was the only thing I had going for me at the time. Dating a player on the team would not have been a good move. If it didn't work out, it would be awkward." It still would be because this was just a dream. She had to return to work and in that reality, she wouldn't be dating an NHL superstar.

"Except it was awkward anyway. Because I didn't know who you were and we wasted all that time."

So he said. It still bothered her, though. She believed he

had this condition—and there were plenty of other reasons why her identity was a mystery to him. But she couldn't help feeling ... unremarkable. Ordinary and discardable, and Erik's explanation didn't make her feel better about that.

Andrew had passed her over, tossed her aside for someone shinier. Deep down, she knew Erik was different but it was still better to be careful.

"I'm not looking to date anyone, Erik. Let's not complicate it."

"A holiday fling?" He frowned. "That's all you want?"

"That's all I want."

The words felt weird on her lips. Trusting her instincts enough to let this man into her body again was one thing. She wouldn't be taking any chances with her heart.

After all, hot Swedish goalies were just for Christmas.

12

"I've got him."

Erik picked up Keanu's case with a gentle strength that melted Casey's heart, but then so many of this man's actions over the last twenty-four hours could be described this way. He had a solidity about him that wasn't forced or fake. Over the years, he had grown into his power and he never let it dominate, except in a way that guaranteed her pleasure.

"If you want to go ahead, I won't mind. Honestly."

Erik closed the door of her car, then beeped the alarm on his own, parked right behind it. He had offered to give her a ride to the Orphan Rebel Christmas at Bren St. James's so she could drink without worry, but now she was second-guessing the plan.

"Perhaps you don't want us to be seen together?" He cocked his head in challenge, but he also seemed amused. As if he expected her to play it this way.

"It's not that—it's just ... well, it immediately puts some sort of label on it, doesn't it? When people spend the holidays together, it attaches importance to it. More than it might deserve." Nuts, this was coming out all wrong.

He shrugged. "It is merely lunch. Surely you are strong enough to endure a bunch of smug smirks and silly looks while I feel you up under the table."

She opened her mouth to explain better but was interrupted as something—or someone—entered her sightline.

Andrew stood outside the door of her apartment building, his expression as dark as the bile she felt surging in her gut.

"Merry Christmas, Casey."

"What are you doing here?" He should be in Winnetka with his parents, just a few miles down the road. Miles she would be happier to see between them.

He lifted his hand, wrapped around the handles of a shopping bag. "My sister had a gift for you so I thought I'd drop by."

On Christmas Day? "How did you know I'd be here?" Most likely, her parents had told him, probably mentioned she'd be all alone with her cat. "Never mind. I can't stop to talk. I'm on my way somewhere."

Then something amazing happened.

Erik took her hand. It was a small thing, a big thing, all points in between. It was everything.

Andrew's eyes widened as if he had just realized she was with someone, someone special. He had called a couple of times over the last year angling for game tickets. Fool that she was, she had given them to him. Purely to show she wasn't wallowing, that she had moved on, but now she realized it looked differently to him.

Andrew thought she still carried a torch, and once upon a time, she might have agreed. Except standing here with Erik's solid strength beside her, she realized that Andrew was very much the past. Even when they were together, he had been historical.

"You're Erik Jorgenson! What are you doing here?"

"I'm with Casey."

"You're with—" A trout-mouthed Andrew flashed a look at her, to their joined hands, then back to Erik. "Like *with* Casey?"

Erik turned to her. "Does 'with' mean something different in English depending on the inflection?"

Depending on the asshole speaking it. Erik didn't wait for her answer, just redirected to Andrew whose mouth was still dropped in a way that Casey was starting to enjoy.

"Unless the meaning of the word has changed," Erik said, steel in his voice, "then you can assume it means how it sounds."

Andrew blinked at that, turned to her. "Now I see why you were obsessed with getting that job."

"I applied for that job because it suited my skill set. And it was your idea that I leave my then job because you thought our relationship would hinder your path to partner."

"Babe, I thought we'd ironed all that out." He threw a quick look at Erik, one of those *women, huh*, glances that was supposed to elicit bro sympathy.

Erik's response was wonderfully dismissive. He turned to Casey. "We need to get going." And then he released her hand and patted her on the ass.

If there was any doubt, that little burst of machismo would have settled it. Normally, she would be annoyed at that kind of behavior but it was nice to be claimed by a hot hockey hunk in front of her asshole ex, even if it was the kind of ridiculous territory-marking that Keanu would have rolled his eyes at.

She held out her hand toward Andrew. "Tell Nancy it was very kind of her to think of me. I'll give her a call after the holiday." She had always gotten along with Andrew's sister, though she wondered why she would use her brother as a go-between. She knew exactly what Casey thought of him.

"I hoped we could talk," Andrew said.

"I'm afraid not. We're late for a party."

Frowning, Andrew placed the bag in her hand, his fingers brushing hers. He held her gaze, questioning what was happening here. As if he found it so difficult to comprehend.

What did that say about how he had thought of her all these years? She was the backup, the Plan B, the second- or more likely fifth-best option. She wasn't the kind of girl to win a hot, rich pro-athlete who could have anyone he wanted.

That's what Andrew thought, and a part of her agreed.

But she refused to show it. Pride reared in her chest and she walked right by him into her building.

CASEY'S APARTMENT was cute with fun art on the walls but distinctly lacking in holiday decoration or the Winter village department.

"Are you okay?" He placed Keanu down and opened the carrier to let him run around. He immediately jumped on the sofa, probably glad to be home in his space.

"I'm fine," she called from the bedroom. She sounded unsure. Whatever that guy had done, it wounded her confidence.

He headed toward her voice and stood at the open door. Casey was pulling dresses out of her closet.

"This lunch is probably dressy, right? I mean, Christmas

with the Chases, so of course it is. And God knows I wouldn't want to show up looking like I didn't belong." She threw a dress on the floor, grabbed another one, ripped it off a hanger and held it up. Two seconds later, it went the way of its closet-mate. The floor and bed were soon littered with piles of fabric.

"I'm sure what you're wearing now is fine."

She shot him a sharp look. "This stupid sweater?"

It looked really cute. He'd already spent time feeling her up in it this morning. "*That* stupid sweater."

Her face crumpled and she sat on the bed, her head in her hands. "I'm sorry. I'm just a bit on edge."

He sat beside her after he moved one of the dresses. "You have nothing to apologize for. Fuckface threw you off your game."

She looked up. "How did you know his nickname?"

"He looks like a natural fuckface. I may have problems recognizing regular faces but fuckfaces are always as clear as day. He may as well have it tattooed on his forehead."

Her smile made his heart thump, then the loss of it made it sink.

"It's been over a year. I shouldn't be so upset but I feel like I was having a lovely time with you and he's polluted it just by being here."

"Why did he come over? Does he want you back?"

"God, no. My parents probably told him I'm alone and miserable, so he came to twist the knife."

"Your parents talk to him?"

"Oh, I'm not going down that road. He can do no wrong in their eyes even when he's been an asshole to their only daughter."

That was horrible. No wonder she was so unsure of herself. Not even her parents were in her corner.

"Can I be honest about something?" she asked.

"Always."

"I don't miss Andrew all that much. But I do miss his family. They were nice to me and I felt included, which is a silly reason to want to stay with someone."

"It's not. We all want to belong. When I moved here, that was the hardest thing, being away from my family. I formed a new one with the guys, though it's worrisome that I could be traded out and lose all that."

"You're easy to like, Erik. You'd have no problem making friends wherever you go." It hovered between them—the uncertainty of being with a pro-hockey player. After seven years with the Rebels, he often wondered if he might be sent on his way at any time. Any woman who wanted him for real would have to be willing to upend her life if he got the call.

It was a lot to expect from a relationship in its budding stage. From what he could tell, Casey wasn't looking for anything deep, and if she was he might not be a good bet.

She raised an eyebrow. "Speaking of making friends, don't think I didn't notice that ass grab."

"He might be a fuckface but he has a nice ass."

"Erik!" Her giggle lit up his life.

"That's more like it." He leaned in to kiss her and she accepted his overture with such sweetness that he was instantly hard.

Twenty minutes later, they were naked, sweaty, and barely sated on a pile of dresses on her bed.

"We're late for lunch," she said, her hand on his chest drawing lazy circles. He liked how owned that made him feel.

"Would it be so terrible if we didn't go?"

Her eyes flew wide. "Really? You don't want to go somewhere with free food?"

He curled a finger in her hair. "Nothing would give me greater pleasure than to show up at a group event with you on my arm and tell everyone we are late because we were having hot, earth-moving sex. But another part of me is thinking I don't need the Orphan Christmas lunch this year."

She rubbed a thumb along his cheekbone. "Because you're not hungry?"

"I'm always hungry. But I don't need it because I'm not an orphan. I have someone to spend it with."

A lovely blush suffused her cheeks. "You want to spend the day with me?"

How could she doubt herself so much? Fuckface needed to pay.

"And Keanu. Let's not forget him."

"That's more consideration than he'd give you."

"If it's too much pressure, then I understand. It's a special day and you had other plans."

Casey had been very clear that this was a holiday fling only. Was there a chance he could persuade her differently? They had lost seven years, all this time he could have been getting to know her. How she took her coffee. What movies she liked. Where she was ticklish. What made her laugh, turned her on, brought tears to her eyes. He had missed out on that.

They had missed out on that.

Twice he had fallen hard and it turned out to be the same woman. The universe must surely be speaking to him.

But for now he would keep within the lines she had drawn.

"The next Rebels game is the night after tomorrow. Let me worship this body until we have to return to work."

"But we can't have sex twenty-four/seven!"

"Challenge accepted. We will take breaks for eating, drinking songs, and maybe a Christmas episode or two of *The Office*." He cupped her face. "Can we spend Christmas Day together, Casey Higgins, just the two of us and Keanu?"

"Erik Jorgensen, I'd love to spend Christmas Day with you, but I have one request."

"Anything."

"Could we do it at your place? It's just so festive and perfect and I feel like I'm on vacation there."

He understood what she was getting at though he wasn't sure he liked it. She wanted to keep this in the realm of fantasy. To stay safely in a snow globe.

She didn't know it yet but he would eventually smash that. Make her confront what came after the holiday.

Now that he had found her again, he would not be letting go.

13

WHIPPING up his mother's French toast egg mixture the day after Christmas, Erik thought about the soft, curvy bundle of woman in his bed. He had left her there, worn out from the night's (and morning's) exertions and now he was creating sustenance to fuel them for the day ahead.

Christmas Day had been amazing. They had come home from Casey's place and returned to bed, only getting up because Erik was hungry. They dined on leftover ham and sausages then watched episodes of *The Office*. It wasn't all sex, salt, and sitcoms—they also talked about their lives, their careers, their families. Erik had prompted her about her past with Fuckface, but she didn't take the bait. He got the impression she wanted to keep their time together conflict-free, avoiding any harsh vibes or deep thoughts. He would have welcomed that access to her heart, but he understood that she was wary of letting him in.

His phone buzzed with a text from Theo.

> Need me to bring anything to brunch?

Brunch? What the—shit. Brunch!

> **ERIK**
> Just yourself.

THEO
You forgot about brunch, didn't you?

> **ERIK**
> No, I didn't. See you at—

He checked the time. Already 9 a.m. In the past, he usually had the guys over around eleven.

> Noon.

THEO
Fine, I'll be there by 11. We're driving back from Saugatuck so I'll drop the fam off and head over to yours.

This is what happened when your mind was blanked by orgasms and a girl who took up every cell in your brain. You forgot that you were hosting a holiday brunch for an entire hockey team.

He was staring at the interior of his fridge wondering if he had enough Prosecco—he didn't—when he felt a warm, soft weight against his back.

"Morning."

He turned and took her in his arms. Her hair was untamed and holy shit, she was wearing one of his jerseys. His heart grew too large for his chest. He'd always dreamed of having a sweetheart who would do that.

"That looks so hot on you."

She grinned. "I hoped you wouldn't mind. I've always wanted to wear one and there it was, hanging in the closet with five others. First, I had to get over the fact you hang your jerseys—"

"They wrinkle!"

"Then I had to get over myself wondering if it was okay to just put it on. I hope it is."

He kissed her softly. "It is. It so is." And now he was going to ruin it with the news of the day. "We have a problem. The guys are coming over."

"The guys?"

"I forgot that I promised to do a post-holiday brunch for anyone who's in town. I knew I'd have all this food so I planned to share it and then you were here and well, I forgot."

She stiffened in his arms. "Okay, I see."

She had already expressed some reservations about being seen with him in company. He understood he might not be her first choice, so he had no intention of making her uncomfortable.

"You can—"

"I should—"

They stopped and smiled at each other. Hers was nervous and he assumed his was the same. Everything seemed pressurized, like the outside world was on the threshold, about to knock the door down with a sledgehammer.

"I don't want to get in the way," she said, which sounded like she didn't want to be here when a bunch of rowdy guys came over. Now probably wasn't the time to mention that Theo already knew about them and the rumor mill was likely creaking under the weight of a Rebels text thread.

"You could never be in the way. But I understand that you're a private person. They are … a lot." He would love to have her here but he wouldn't push. Things were at a delicate stage.

She stepped out of his arms, creating a hollowness in his chest.

"Anything you need me to do?"

Just stay and be mine forever. "No. Nothing. I need to get to the store and get some booze in. We got through a lot of it yesterday."

She smiled, a little more oomph to it this time.

"I'll let you get on." Then she headed upstairs, and he got to watch his number walking away from him.

Erik parked in his garage and shut the door with the remote. He had thirty minutes before the guys descended and he already saw how it would go. He'd be spending more time in the kitchen hosting than eating. But he was a caregiver. It couldn't be helped.

Usually he'd be looking forward to guy-time, but today he just wanted to chill with a certain curly-haired goddess and her cranky cat. He hated how he'd left things with Casey. He'd had such a magical couple of days with her and now it felt, not exactly over, but like he was back to square one, trying to woo her.

Balancing a case of Prosecco under his arm, he opened the side door from the garage to the house.

Bublé's "It's Beginning to Look a Lot Like Christmas" was playing.

The scent of cooking wafted into his nostrils—was that the meatballs he had already prepared simmering in a bath of delicious tomato sauce?

A plaintive mewl sounded at his feet. Keanu looked up at him and growled like a dog.

"What's going on, Keanu?"

The cat hissed and headed into the kitchen. Following, Erik marveled at the sight he saw. Women. Action. Food. All of his favorite things.

And his most favorite of all: Casey in his Well Hung apron directing traffic.

"Tara, put the rödkål on the table," she ordered while attending to what looked like mini caprese salads on toothpicks.

"Which one is the roadkill?"

"The cabbage and apple salad. It's on the second shelf in the fridge. We can start putting out the cold dishes now." She added a basil leaf to her creation.

"Hey, Fish." Mia waved at him with the hand not stirring what looked like a pitcher of Mimosas. "Happy holidays!"

"Same to you. Is Cal here?"

"He's around. He was getting to know Keanu a while back."

Casey met his gaze. "Hi, there." Something about the way she looked at him revved his engine and melted his heart. He couldn't believe she had stayed.

"I didn't expect you to still be here."

"I know you didn't ask, but I didn't think you'd mind if we put a holiday brunch together for the team. I mean, you've done all the work but we're adding a few extras." She cocked her head and took him in. "Have I screwed up?"

He took her in his arms and kissed the breath out of her.

"We'll take that as a no," Tara said as she walked by with the rödkål. "Hey, Jorgenson, will Dex O'Malley be coming?"

Mia chimed in. "Probably already did with the twins last night. Zing!"

"He was invited," Erik said, still unable to take his eyes off his girl. "Don't know if he'll make it." He squeezed Casey's waist. "Could I see you in the living room?"

"Sure."

He led her by the hand until they were out of earshot. The fire was lit and several of the plates were set out on the big dining table, the perfect Swedish julbord. Assorted side tables had been moved around so they were more conveniently placed for people to sit in comfort and eat.

"You stayed."

"Is this okay? I don't have to stay—the girls and I can head out before everyone gets here."

"No, you should stay. All of you. I only invited the guys but Remy has already texted to say Harper and his little ones are coming over with him. And Theo said Elle wanted to stop in to say hi as well with Hatch. It seems all the WAGs and offspring will be here."

"So not a complete sausage-fest."

"There will be enough prinskorv to go around."

"No sharing your sausage, Jorgenson." She snaked her arms around his neck and kissed him until he moaned like a fool.

She stayed. Now he had to do everything in his power to ensure she never left.

14

Casey had been waylaid.

Sadie Yates, Gunnar Bond's girlfriend, had joined Mia and Tara, and the group had cornered her near Christmas tree prime to give her the third degree. She'd managed to escape most of the questions earlier because it was eyes down, work to be done, but now she had no choice but to submit to the girl squad interrogation.

"And there I was thinking you had something against Erik, but it looks like I had it all wrong." Mia shook her head. "Why did I have it all wrong, Tara?"

Tara tapped a long nail against Casey's shoulder. "Because this one gave us the distinct impression that she found Erik to be immature and inconsiderate and a lot of other multi-syllabic words that painted a picture of degeneracy and assholery. Why would you do that? What have you been keeping from us, Higgins?"

Casey swallowed. "It's a long story which I can't go into now. But the bottom line is that we hooked up years ago and —" She stopped. No way did she want to tell people about

Erik's condition. "Anyway, yada yada, he's been trying to be nice to me for a while and I wanted to make him suffer."

"And now the penance is complete?" Sadie grinned. "Groveled on his knees, I hope."

"It's where those goaltenders do their best work," murmured Tara.

"So, are you guys just having fun or is there more to it?"

Casey bit her lip at Mia's question that cut right to the heart of it. What could she say that wouldn't jinx it? She had packed her fantasies about Erik away for years and now it was like opening a hope chest and pulling out old diaries and treasured memories.

She wanted this a little too much.

"Just fun." The words sounded wrong but it was far too soon for them to sound right.

"Well, don't wring him out too much," Tara said. "I might have plans for him later."

"What plans?"

Mia glared at Tara. "Don't listen to her, she's teasing."

"I'm making a list," Tara sang softly, "checking it twice. Gonna find out who's naughty or … *reallygoodinbed*. Tara Becker is ready … to get down." Tara's ambitions to grab herself a Rebel trophy husband were well-known. She wasn't the least bit subtle and now took her friends' teasing about it in good spirit. "Just kidding about Erik. He's adorable but a little too wholesome for little ole me."

Wholesome wouldn't really apply to how he had woken her up this morning. She kept that to herself.

"Dex O'Malley, on the other hand. This TMZ business is kind of wild." Tara held up her phone, showing a shot of the new Rebel rolling out of a club with a different supermodel. The manho energy singed the screen.

"Harper won't like to see that kind of press, especially

with a player on IR," Casey said. "He needs to be resting up." Dex had been traded in a month before but hadn't played yet owing to an elbow injury. He hadn't shown up for lunch either—probably sleeping off the night's excesses.

"Oh, I'm sure your new generalissimo will lay down the law." Tara shuddered. "He's not invited to this, is he?"

Mia grinned. "Why, planning to insult the man to his face this time?"

Tara's mouth twisted sourly. "I didn't know he was listening in! And he is, old—um, older. Fills out a suit well enough, but not my type at all. Now, Sexy Dexy can shake my tree anytime." Tara froze at whatever she saw on Mia's face. "Oh fuck, he's standing right behind me, isn't he?"

Casey turned and sure enough, there was the Rebels' new GM on another stealth approach. As he didn't officially start until January 1, she was surprised to see him, but not as surprised as Tara, who spun expertly on her very high heels and got off a volley before Fitz even opened his mouth.

"Listen, Spock, I can't help it if you're always sneaking up on people and hearing things you shouldn't!"

Fitz looked baffled. "Spock?"

"Because of your big ears, eavesdropper."

"Ah, but how else am I gonna find out all the gossip? Just pretend I'm not here and tell me what you really think. Or I guess it doesn't matter—you'd tell me anyway."

With a flick of her hair, Tara delivered her most dead-eyed look. "I have no opinion of you whatsoever."

"Well, I heard a couple in there," he drawled in that deep Georgian tone, eyes twinkling like the lights on the tree behind them. "One, I'm geriatric. Two, I'm old."

Sadie murmured, "They actually mean the same thing, so just one opinion."

"But nice to hear I fill out a suit well even if I'm not your type."

"Not everyone can be someone's type," Tara said, coloring. "I'm sure you do admirably with whatever you've got going on." She looked exceptionally uncomfortable. Usually she was impossible to shame.

"Keep digging, you'll haul yourself out eventually." With a wink at her, he went on his way.

Tara shut her eyes, inhaled deeply, then opened them again. "That man is so rude, listening to private conversations!" She arced a haughty gaze over the group and said louder, "And I don't care who hears it."

Casey exchanged an amused glance with Mia. "I think he was very polite under the circumstances. You did call him geriatric and then implied he had a tough time getting dates."

"Might be easier to manage a doddering senior than a slippery fish like Dex O'Malley," Mia said.

Casey giggled. "With Dex, you'd need to fight the twins for him, assuming they're still in the frame."

Tara beamed, back on the safer territory of how to use her considerable wiles. "I could take them both with my hands tied behind my back. One pop and those plastic puppies they call breasts will deflate, throwing off their center of gravity."

While Tara launched into her latest plan to snag the attention of an eligible NHL star, Casey's attention wandered, anxious to latch onto Erik. He had looked so surprised to find her here, helping out, and she hoped she hadn't overstepped. She wouldn't want him to think she was assuming a larger than necessary role in his life. After all, they were just a holi-hang (upgraded from holi-bang).

But he also seemed glad to see her taking such an active part in the brunch.

Ah, there. He was seated on the sofa beside Cade who held his baby girl, Rosie. And then, as if she had wished it, Cade placed the baby in Erik's arms and the perfect tableau was set. His strong, sweater-wrapped arms cradled the baby, ensuring her safety.

But then this man had the safest hands in the NHL.

Casey loved seeing him like this. Erik was born to be a family man. He came from a strong, nurturing background so a wife and kids would have that lovely extended family to support them. He'd bought this big house, clearly hoping to fill it with love. It was a lot of square footage for one man, but might be still too small for a heart as large as Erik's.

He snagged her gaze just then with a smile that slayed her and made her realize that she was invested here.

Thoroughly, deeply, stupidly invested.

"Well, look what we have here." Remy stood at the door to the kitchen, wearing an ugly sweater and a shit-eating grin.

Erik had stopped off to grab another plate of rye bread. "Sorry I missed the Christmas Day lunch."

"Heard you were otherwise occupied. Someone else missed you, though."

A blond sprite-slash-terror crashed into Erik.

"Where were you yesterday?" Giselle was one of Remy and Harper's five-year-old twins and for some reason known only to her, had taken a liking to Erik a few months ago. Luckily, he could tell her apart from her sister Amelie, as Giselle liked to wear her hair in braids.

"You missed me, lilla gumman?"

"What does that mean?"

"It means 'sweet girl.'" It actually meant sweet *little* girl, but he had enough experience with nephews and nieces to know the smallest ones objected to anything that hinted at their smallness.

"I wanted to show you the new skates Daddy got me."

"Well, next time. Or we can go skating together."

"I'll score goals on you!"

"You sure will, ma cherie," Remy said, laughing. "Jorgenson's gettin' old, bless his slowing reflexes."

Casey walked in and waved at Remy. "I have a few small things for the girls that I meant to bring over, though I imagine they have everything they've ever wanted."

Remy grinned. "They are DuPre women. Never satisfied."

"Hey Giselle, did you want to see the Christmas village?" At Giselle's enthusiastic nodding, Casey winked at Erik and took the little girl by the hand.

As he watched them go, his chest felt both tight and hot. All afternoon they'd been working as a team, making sure his guests were fed and watered, and it had felt so good to have her close by. Only when Remy nudged him did he realize he'd lost a few awkward moments and brain cells while he dreamed about filling his house with a gaggle of little girls. Blue eyes, some blonde, some dark, all curls.

"You've got it bad, mon ami."

Christ, had he said any of that out loud? Or did he just look lovesick?

"I'm trying not to overplay my hand. She's sort of skittish."

"Know what that's like."

Erik tried to imagine Harper ever being wary around

Remy. She put on a good act, that was for sure. Maybe Casey was the same.

Remy rubbed his hands together. "How can I help?"

"Cooking's already done. You're just a guest here."

Remy would not be deterred, so Erik put him to work making Sazerac cocktails.

A few minutes later, Harper appeared beside him at the counter with surprising covertness for a woman who spent most of her days in heels. "Erik."

He had lived here for five years and hosted a holiday lunch event annually. This was the first time Harper had ever stopped by. "Ma'am."

Remy coughed and muttered something unintelligible in French.

Harper glared at him, but when she spoke, it was to Erik. "You're sassin' me now, Jorgenson?"

"Don't know what that means." *Lie.*

Narrowed eyes assessed him. "I haven't had a chance to talk to Casey yet but I assume her presence here with a smile on her face means that things are going well."

"Might be."

"Coy doesn't suit you, Swede."

"It's going better than I could have hoped."

"What's that for?" She pointed at his face.

"We ran into her ex yesterday. He dropped a gift over at her place. I didn't like him."

Harper's look said, *well, you wouldn't, would you?*

"He made her ... doubt herself." Along with all the possibility of them, Erik and Casey.

She squeezed his arm. "Erik, this is okay. Every relationship comes with baggage." She shot a look at Remy who had a well-worn smirk on his lips. "It's how you deal with the baggage that defines you."

"I like her." *Like* seemed too mild, so he added, "A lot." It still felt shockingly inadequate. "Bränt barn skyr elden."

Harper frowned.

"Burnt child shuns the fire," Erik explained, though it didn't translate well. What was the phrase in English? Once bitten, twice shy. "I think she's scared about starting something because of what happened before with her ex."

At least he would rather attribute it to her past experience than any fault in his own makeup. Swedes subscribed to the philosophy of Lagom: everything in moderation, not too much or too little, balance with the world. Part of this was to avoid standing out. He never had and he never tried. He wasn't used to going overboard with anything, and now he wondered if that was his problem. If he needed to be more proactive.

"Erik, if I didn't think this was a good idea—that you and Casey were a good idea—I would not be threatening you with physical violence to ensure that two of my favorite people get together. Of course if all either of you want is something more ... casual, then so be it."

Significant cough from Remy.

Infamous eyebrow arch of disapproval from Harper. "Something to say, DuPre?"

"Wouldn't dream of it, minou."

Erik wished these two would tell him what they really thought.

"What I'm saying," Harper said, "is that I see great potential here and I think you need to have a little more faith."

He wasn't a pessimist by nature. He saw potential in most everything, so why couldn't he see it here?

"I've got to go check on the cat."

Remy frowned. "You have a cat?"

"It's Casey's. He's upstairs, sulking."

Harper's expression went all soft while Remy shook his head. *Smug married people*, as Theo would say, though he was a smug married person himself. Erik left the kitchen to seek out the one creature here that wouldn't give him a hard time.

He put his head around the door of his room. No sign of him. They had stashed him here with his litter box, food, and water for the duration of the party—a couple decision! —so he wouldn't be poked at by the kids. Keanu was much too senior to tolerate that.

Erik dropped to his knees and checked under the bed. A pair of devil eyes shone back at him in the semi-dark.

"I brought you a treat." He offered a sliver of herring, withdrawing his hand as the cat drew closer. But he wasn't an asshole about it. As soon as the cat drew near, Erik let him lick the fishy flesh from his hand.

He picked Keanu up and set him in his lap, expecting him to resist. He remained still.

"You've got the right idea, holing up in here, Keanu."

He took the cat's silence as assent to continue.

"I just want all these people to leave so it can be you, me, and Casey. That's it."

His phone buzzed with a message from his sister, Elsa.

> You still playing house with your honey?

He and Elsa were the closest in age and in the past he had told her more than he probably should have. She liked to use his honesty to torture him.

> **ERIK**
> It's going well, but now I've told you that, it is 100% jinxed.

> **ELSA**
> Give her space. Let it breathe before you show your weirdo side.

> **ERIK**
> Too late.

He thought back on what Harper had said, about baggage. He didn't think he carried much around with him except for his medical condition, which he had adapted to as well as he could. It had delayed his reunion with Casey but now he was back in the game.

He just had to be sure not to scare her off.

15

CASEY'S PHONE buzzed with a text from her mother. Her parents had checked in yesterday with a picture of their holiday lunch on the cruise, so they were having a good time and not missing her in the slightest.

> This could have been you!

What did that mean? She clicked the link her mother provided to ... damn, Facebook and double damn, Andrew's feed.

There they were, the fabulous couple at the law firm holiday party. Cozying up to each other and a couple of the partners, champagne in hand, smiles in place, everything going swimmingly.

The third finger of her left hand all sparkly.

Engaged.

Eight years together, off and on, and Andrew had practically had a heart attack when Casey mentioned marriage.

I want to be in a better financial position, babe. I want to give you everything you deserve.

Instead he'd taken all the love she gave him and crushed it underfoot.

She closed her eyes and waited for the tears to come but nada. She'd spent the last year marinating in a bitter brew of social media stalking, dreams of what could have been, and recognition that her bank account—and spirit—were poorer for having met Andrew.

That was probably why he stopped by her place yesterday, wanting to gloat about his engagement only to have his thunder stolen by Erik being so adorable.

Today the adorableness continued with the man holding baby Rosie like a natural and charming the braids off Giselle, who later told her while they looked at the Winter Village that Erik was her favorite of all the players because he had the best hair and he was funny. Casey had to agree. More than that, he was a total sweetheart.

Her heart thrummed. Maybe it wasn't as hardened as she liked to think. She wanted to see her Swedish hunk, feel his arms around her, know that after everyone left tonight she could eat pie and watch silly TV shows and let herself be cared for.

No trace of him in the kitchen or the den. She headed upstairs—it was time she checked on Keanu anyway—and stopped on the landing because she heard her name.

"So, you and Casey, man?"

That sounded like Tate Kazminski, one of the Rebels defensemen. He must be talking to Erik, and that was confirmed at the sound of the next voice.

Whatever Erik said was too low for her to hear. She strained her ears so hard she almost pulled a muscle.

Tate's voice again. "So you managed to figure out what you did to piss her off?"

"It's a long story."

"And now you two are what? Dating?"

"Nah, just a casual thing. No big deal."

Casey's heart dropped. *No big deal.* It was exactly the attitude she had brought to the table—or tried to. Keep it light. Nothing serious. But to hear Erik say it ... hurt.

Of course it was casual. Erik might have given her all that spiel about wanting to make up for the last seven years but that didn't mean anything. Not really.

She stepped back, into the bathroom, seeking a moment of calm. If Erik was truly interested, wouldn't he have confided that in his teammates? His honest directness was one of her favorite things about him. He had known these men for years; surely they shared their hopes and dreams. To be so summarily dismissed sounded at odds with what she had thought might be happening here. Obviously her instincts were all wrong.

She had wanted to be the one in his life, the woman he came home to. But those were starry-eyed notions, the silly dreams of a girl who had no right to them. She had held them inside her heart for so long and for a couple of days, had fooled herself into thinking she was getting a do-over.

That night seven years ago was supposed to end that way. Fantasies should remain buried, taken out only on long, cold nights. Not lived in the warm, wide open.

The brittle shell she'd built to cover her heart had finally hardened into something impenetrable. She could be casual. She could have holi-bangs with hot hockey players. She wasn't Andrew—she didn't need a new model to replace the old. Sure, it was nice to not spend the holiday season alone but Erik was right.

No big deal.

"Casey, you don't have to do all this cleaning."

"I don't mind." She continued scrubbing a pan. They hadn't had much chance to talk while everyone was here. It was hard to be a host and a good partner, or at least Erik didn't really know how to do that. He could do better, though, given the chance.

He placed a hand on her hip and turned her to face him.

"Erik," she said with a smile. "My hands are wet."

"Just your hands?"

She dried them on a dishtowel. "I really should get going."

His heart lurched. "Now?"

"Yes, I need to get Keanu settled back home. He's had a nice little holiday and"—she smiled—"so have I. But now it's back to reality."

Not liking the sound of that. "This isn't real enough for you?"

"Erik, we said it would be just for a few days."

"Yes, but I thought you would still be here, at least until ... I don't know ... longer."

What had he done wrong? He had thought they were a team, putting this brunch together. Okay, so she did most of the work and maybe she was annoyed about that. Only he didn't think so.

"This was lovely," she said. "A really great way to spend Christmas and I'm glad we could keep each other company. But you know, all good things and all that ..."

No, he didn't know. But he had pushed before. In the elevator, in the closet, for lunch, and so much more. He couldn't make her want him. No matter how much he wanted her.

"Did something happen?" There he went, pushing again. He was being too intense, too demanding.

"No, not at all!" She rubbed his arm. "I'm glad I could help out and I'm glad we could clear the air."

Clear the air? They had been doing much more than that over the last few days ... or at least he had assumed so. Sometimes he was accused of being oblivious, so that must be what was happening here. He had misread all the signals.

"I'll drive you home."

"No need! I can call an Uber."

"I'll drive you home. You have all of Keanu's stuff to carry."

"Okay, that's kind of you."

It wasn't kind, at least not to himself. He wanted to prolong his agony like a sap.

Ten minutes later, he pulled up outside her place. On the way over, they had chatted about the game tomorrow, their chances of making the playoffs, a whole bunch of stuff that Erik barely remembered.

Yesterday, they had stopped by her apartment building and run into her ex—was that what this was about? Did she still have feelings for him? A vision of her bedroom littered with dresses popped into Erik's brain, and even though he had used those dresses as a nest for great sex, the reason they were strewn about was still there. She had been upset after seeing that guy, and that might still be on her mind.

He could ask her, but he had already probed enough. "Let me help you."

"Sure." She held onto Keanu in his carrier while Erik grabbed the rest and trooped to the front door of her building. He walked her inside and stopped outside her apartment, laying all Keanu's bits and pieces down because she said it was *fine, just fine, leave it there.*

Dying to get away from him, he supposed.

He wanted to ask again if something had happened, but it would only come off as clingy.

She opened her door and put Keanu inside, then turned to him. Something in her eyes confused the hell out of him.

A sadness that gutted him.

This was all wrong. But he didn't know what to say to make it better. It felt like any words he had would come out mangled.

So he did the only thing he could: he kissed her.

It might not convince her of anything but at least *he* would know he did something.

Surprise parted her lips and yielded him access to the sweetest mouth he had ever tasted. She was the feast to his hunger, the water to his thirst, the comfort to his need. She was everything he had ever wanted.

She pulled back, touching fingertips to her lips. Her eyes blazed with emotion, and for a moment, he thought she would surrender to the thrumming need vibrating between them. Accept that this was meant to be.

But his wishes weren't enough. Hurt was more powerful than hope.

"Thanks for everything, Erik. I'll see you around."

He didn't answer. He could say nothing that would satisfy them both. Instead he watched her take her belongings into her apartment and shut the door on their Yule reunion.

16

"Casey, could you come into my office, please?"

"Sure, Harper."

She grabbed a notebook and pen and headed into the inner sanctum. She loved Harper's office. Decorated in an elegant French style, it had beautiful drapes, comfortable furniture, and candid shots of the team on the walls. Her eyes skimmed over Erik.

Harper was seated on the velvet tufted blue sofa near the window. The coffee service was already set out on the table.

"When did that happen?" Casey usually took care of that for Harper's guests. Not everyone got the treatment though, just the people she wanted to have cozy chats with.

So that's how it is.

"I got here early and took care of it myself." She patted the seat beside her. "Come, have coffee with me."

"But I have the salary caps report to run."

Harper raised an eyebrow. *Trapped.* Casey took a seat and waited while her boss poured and creamed and sugared.

Harper passed her the coffee. "How was your holiday?"

"Well, I saw you twice so I think you know how it was." She shook her head, embarrassed at her snark. "Sorry, that was rude. It was fine."

Better than fine. The most wonderful three days she had ever spent and then it had ended with a whimper. Hers, as she slumped against the door in pain after she let Erik walk away.

"And how are things with my favorite Swede?"

"Fine."

"So, all fine. Back to work, then!"

Casey narrowed her eyes. "Look, I appreciate you trying to … well, I don't know exactly what you're trying to do."

"Put people I like together in a manner that pleases me."

"Sure thing, puppet master."

Harper's lips curved. "Erik's not like the other guys on this team. He's not prone to tantrums, egomania, or overthinking with his dick. Or at least I don't think he is. Maybe you can fill me in on the last one." When Casey didn't respond, Harper plowed on. "I know you had a long relationship that didn't work out and that dating a hockey player seems like a huge step outside your comfort zone. I remember my own reluctance to consider that. So tell me what's on your mind."

Too much, that's what. "Erik and I spent some time together and kept each other company over the holidays. He's kind of lonely, I think. That big house, missing his family, all his friends moving on. I get it. We see the people around us pairing off and wonder, why not us."

She was under no illusions that Erik wanted more than a warm body to comfort him during his favorite time of the year. After all the soul-searching, that was the conclusion she had landed on. Erik liked her well enough, but if she let it go any further, it would kill her when it ended for real.

Because what happened wasn't already real enough? The hurt she felt now certainly seemed as real as any past or future imagined pain. If this was only a fraction, she wasn't interested in the whole thing.

"It was nice to not be on my own. Erik feels the same way. We're friends who hung out and ate and drank and"—fucked and sang drinking songs and told stories and watched TV—"enjoyed each other's company. That's it, Harper. You can stop trying to push us together now."

Harper assessed her. "Why were you always snippy with him before?"

"Snippy? I've never been snippy in my life."

The boss waited. Waited some more. And was rewarded when Casey blurted out, "I—I met him before. Years ago. And—it doesn't matter!"

"He forgot you because of the face thing."

Casey blinked. "You know about that?"

"Pretty much the only person in the team org who does. He's very private about it. Worried it makes him seem less than whole."

"There's nothing less than whole about him. Not at all."

Harper nodded. "So you believed him when he said he didn't recognize you?"

"Yes." Yet a part of her still felt slighted by it. As if she couldn't emerge from the sea of unrecognizable faces and be the one that Erik remembered. The one that stood out. "But even believing that, it still ... hurts, I suppose. He was so apologetic about it. I don't want him to have to keep apologizing, not for something out of his control." She thought about it for a moment, grateful that Harper waited patiently. "But with my ex, I always felt like I wasn't the most important thing in the world to him. That in another life, he wouldn't have chosen me. Then when he had this other life, the one he wanted, the one I helped him get, he realized I was superfluous to requirements. He had always come first"—in more ways than the obvious—"and now I want to put myself first for a while. I've seen how it works with pro-athletes. It's all about them, their needs, their careers. I've been with someone who put his career before me. I can't let myself get in too deep with another guy who won't remember me or could be moving on."

During that outburst, Harper had listened closely and now Casey waited for some wise words from the woman who had seen it all.

"You're right," Harper finally said. "You shouldn't settle for some guy who isn't going to treat you as the center of the universe."

Okay. Casey went quiet but it didn't have the same effect as when Harper did it to her. No more searing wisdom was emerging from Harper's mouth.

"I should get back to work." Casey sipped her cooling coffee and put it down on the tray. "I'll take care of this."

"Leave it for the moment. I'd like to sit and think for a bit."

"Sure." Casey stood, not sure what had happened but knowing this felt unfinished. It all did. "Erik's a great guy. I know that."

Harper smiled in agreement. Still not a word from the woman who could rarely shut up.

Casey went on. "The time I spent with him over the holiday was really special. I know he was lonely but I still felt like he cared I was there."

Nod from Harper. Damn, this was how she handled contract negotiations. The woman was a master at the bluff.

"Could you just tell me what you think?"

The Rebels boss touched a hand to her throat. "You want my opinion?"

"I know you have one."

"I do, but I'm trying to not fill your brain with my ideas. This is your life, Casey. You've set standards for yourself and any man who comes into it. He needs to put you first, plain and simple. Only you can say what that looks like in reality."

Casey nodded, not feeling any better after a girl-talk with the boss. She should feel better, shouldn't she?

"Thanks for listening, Harper." She turned to leave.

"No problem. Just one more thing." Harper held her gaze, direct and true. "I would rather be forgotten by a man as good as Erik Jorgenson than remembered by some of the men I've been with."

Erik sat on the bench in the locker room and started to unstrap his pads. Morning skate had gone okay.

Fuck, he was lying to himself, now? It had gone terribly. Focus was hard to come by the last few days. He had let in a couple of goals during the game the night before last but luckily the Rebels offensive line was on top of it and made up for his mistakes.

"What's up, Fish?" Cade sat down beside him, his brow lined with concern. "You seem out of sorts."

"I'm—okay."

Cade frowned at him.

"Fell out with his girl, didn't he?" Dex O'Malley pulled off his jersey. "That's the rumor."

Dex was newer to the team and Erik didn't know him well. No one did. Yet he had somehow fallen nose-deep into the Rebels groove, the one where everyone was in everyone else's business. "Where did you hear that?"

"I dunno. Someone said something." He made a flapping gesture with his fingers to indicate gossip. "Just forget her. Plenty more fish, Fish."

Cade stared after Dex as he headed into the shower, then turned to Erik. "Wouldn't take advice from the guy who has shares in boner palaces. Did something happen between you and Casey?"

"There is no me and Casey. We're just friends." He hoped they were that at the very least.

Theo called out, "Sure ya are. Yet there she was acting like the hostess with the mostess at your Swedish bro brunch. Looked right at home."

"She was helping me out, that's all. Nothing more."

Cal, Theo, and Cade all shared baffled looks at Erik's gloomy tone. Cal spoke up. "You sure?"

"She's not interested in me and why would she be? Of course she's not going to want to get serious with a guy who can't even recognize the woman he fell for years ago. Who would want to be with someone like that?"

He threw one of his leg pads at his cubby. Then the other. Rage waved through him, building to a familiar peak. He used to get angry with himself as a kid because of how inadequate he felt. He had learned workarounds and coped as well as he could, only now his defect had cost him dearly. Casey didn't trust him because underlying all of this was their history—the one where he failed to see what was staring him in the face.

He had fallen hard for this woman but his brain couldn't make it work.

Cade placed a hand on his shoulder. "Erik, what are you talking about? What happened years ago?"

"I met Casey before, one night years ago in the Empty Net. You were with me. At the end of our first season together."

"Years ago?" Cade rubbed his chin. "Wait, the redhead you went nuts over because you lost that napkin with her number. What was her name? I want to say Bozo but that can't be right."

"Coco. Her name was Coco." He had talked Cade's ear off about it at the time. "But it wasn't her real name. It was Casey and when I found her again—here of all places, right under my nose!—I didn't recognize her."

"Aw, shit, Fish!" Theo shook his head. "That's why she was mad at you? Did you two ...?" He made a gesture that shouldn't be used in mixed company.

"Yes! But I didn't forget her. Not at all. I have a problem with recognizing people."

"Prosopagnosia," someone said.

Erik looked up at Reid Durand, who had appeared out of nowhere and dropped that gem. "Yes, that's it. How did you know?"

Reid shrugged. "I ran into you once at Walgreens and you asked me how the baby was, but then you switched real quick to asking about my dog. Figured you thought I was Kershaw for a second. I have a cousin with it. He says it's a pain in the ass."

"Wait, what's this about?" Cal asked.

"Face blindness," Erik said. "I can't always recognize someone until they speak."

Theo looked confused. "So you ran into Duracell and thought he was me? In the glaring neon light of Walgreens? But I'm ten times more fucking handsome than this dude!"

"If he'd seen my ass first," Durand said, "he probably

would have known immediately that it wasn't you. You can see yours from space, Superglutes."

Cade waved. "Could we maybe quit worrying about whether Kershaw's ass is more recognizable than his face and get back to the issue at hand?"

Everyone returned to staring at Erik, no doubt recalibrating their past interactions through the filter of this new information.

Cal sniffed. "So should we wear name tags or something? Make things more accessible?"

Cade shook his head. "Not that kind of help, Foreskin. Or maybe ..." He checked in with Erik.

"No, I don't need that. I have my ways of figuring things out."

Cade looked relieved. "So you're doing fine, except for not recognizing the woman who blew your mind years ago. But she understands, right? You explained it?"

"I did. And she says she understands. But she made it clear she wants to keep it casual."

"Mia said she had some bad experience with her last boyfriend," Cal said. "Sounds like she's not ready for another commitment."

"What's that got to do with it?" Theo asked. "Why are all these women assuming past performance is indicative of future results? Erik just has to convince her that he's the one for her."

Foreman looked skeptical. "Sure, just blow in and demand she play to his tune. Relationships are a two-way street, Kershaw. Not that you'd know given that your strategy to get into one is to knock your girl up so she has no choice but to spend time with you."

Theo scoffed. "Yeah, listen to the guy who's had how many girlfriends?"

"More than you, all of whom I have remained on good terms with. Because I treat every lady of my acquaintance with respect and reverence—"

"Even when he's dumping them in a way that makes them think it was their idea all along."

Cal glared at Reid Durand, who had put that out there. The usually surly Canuck picked up the conversation.

"Fish, don't take advice from these knuckleheads. Have you told Casey what's on your mind?"

"I was worried about coming on too strong. Being too intense." Erik scrubbed his face. "I like her. Hell, I'm crazy about her. But she doesn't trust easily."

"So, that would be a no, then." Cade grinned at him. "Durand's got the right idea. Tell her you're interested in more and if it's not meant to be, then you'll know and can move on."

Reid added, "If you like this girl, don't waste time or let her think for a second you might be lukewarm in your interest. You let her slip through your fingers once. You want to lose your shot again?"

Erik stared at Reid, who had recently found happiness and opened up, not just with Kennedy, his girlfriend. The last couple of months had seen him improve in his team dynamics as well. At the beginning of the season, he would have sneered at the conversation and kept his mouth shut.

Reid was right. Erik needed to step up to the goalmouth and defend his territory.

17

Erik was late.

Fitz's assistant was off so Casey was handling his schedule as well as Harper's. He had asked to meet all the players in fifteen minute slots and Erik should have been here five minutes ago. Usually he arrived at least ten minutes early for any meeting with Harper. She hoped he was okay.

And then suddenly he was there, his eyes a little sad. She opened her mouth to say something, but Fitz appeared at the door and gestured Erik inside his office.

Damn.

She shuttered her eyes as the door closed. Three days since she had seen him. Three days of self-recrimination and tears and feeling like she had screwed up a real chance at happiness here.

The door opened again after fifteen minutes. For a second she thought Erik would walk by the desk when he stopped.

"Hi, Casey."

"Hey! How are you?"

He smiled and her heart boomed at the sight. "Good. How is Keanu?"

"Heartbroken. Misses all the wandering space at your house."

"He's welcome to visit anytime. Take a vacation at Chez Jorgenson."

She chuckled. "He'd like that."

And then she ran out of things to say.

And so, apparently, did he.

The phone rang, but she would rather stare in awkward silence at this beautiful man than be supposedly saved by the bell.

Unfortunately the phone had other ideas. "I'm sorry, I need to …" She gestured to the phone and picked it up. "Good morning, how can I help you?"

Someone spoke but Casey didn't hear a word of it because Erik was still there, looming over her desk. He wasn't walking away!

She blinked as she realized it was Ford Callaghan calling to say he'd be late for his appointment. "No problem, Ford. Got it. See you later."

She hung up and smiled up at the Rebels goalie, who was waiting for her to finish. That was Erik all over, patient and solid, and realizing this opened her heart wide.

"I have something for you."

Surprise lit up his face. "For me?"

"I ordered it, hoping it would arrive the day of the brunch but it took a few days." She reached for the bag at the side of her chair, removed a wrapped box, and placed it on the desk.

He ran a finger along the edge, then over the curl of the ribbon. She imagined that same finger crooked in her hair and had to blink away the emotions it raised.

"Should I open it now or wait until next year?"

"Now." As he tore at the packaging, she suddenly got nervous. "It's not a big deal, just a gag gift, really."

"It will make me gag?"

"No, that's not what I—oh, just open it!"

He opened the box, pulled apart the tissue paper, and held up a "I'm Dreaming of a Dwight Christmas" sweater. He was a fan of the show, and of Dwight Schrute in particular, so she thought it would make him happy. She loved nothing more than seeing this man happy.

"This is perfect."

"You can wear it next year or—" He was already removing his jacket and peeling off his sweatshirt. "Now. You can wear it now."

She was too nervous to enjoy the sight of a shirtless Erik Jorgenson, all those golden muscles, perfectly packed and rippling as he maneuvered the sweater over his head, right there in the Rebels' front office. At least she assumed that was what was happening. Her eyes had turned ridiculously blurry.

"It fits," he said with a grin, his hair electrified with static. "What do you think?"

Standing and rounding her desk, eliminating that final barrier, she fought back the press of tears in her throat and reached up to smooth his hair.

"God Jul, Erik," she whispered. "I know it's over, but—"

He grasped her wrist, probably because he didn't want her to touch him. She had hurt this wonderful man and it was understandable that he wanted nothing more to do with her.

Yet he held on, raised her hand to his lips, and planted a small, yet significant kiss to her trembling palm.

"It isn't over, Casey. Christmas in Sweden goes until

Tjugondag jul. That's the twentieth day of Christmas, also known as Knut's Day."

"When's that?" she whispered.

"January 13th. And before that is trettondedag jul, which is the thirteenth day of Christmas on January 6th. There are still many holidays to be celebrated."

"And what about us, Erik?" *Are we over?*

"That's up to you."

"I thought ... I thought this was casual for you."

His eyes burned with that Jorgenson intensity she was starting to recognize. "I am clearly terrible at this dating and relationships business."

"How do you make that out?"

"If I can spend all that time with you, feed you and fuck you and try to treat you the way a woman as amazing as you deserves, and still have you think it's only casual? That you still believe every second I spent with you didn't mean the world to me?"

Her heart sped up. "But I heard you talking to Kazminski and saying that. Telling him we were no big deal."

He looked baffled. "Kaz? You think I'd tell that guy anything? He's the biggest gossip in the NHL. You know he blabbed to the press about Durand's sex fast? He is not to be trusted with any sensitive information."

"So you ... lied to him?"

"Of course I did! I didn't want anyone to know how bad I had it until we were on a more sure footing. I've fallen on my ass with you too many times. If it got back to you that I was gaga over you, I might scare you off." He entwined his fingers in hers. "I'm scaring you now, aren't I?"

"No. Well, sort of, but only because this is scary stuff. Relationships are scary. And I let the fear take over. Thing is, Andrew—"

"Fuckface."

"Yes, Fuckface. He got engaged to the woman who replaced me and I heard about it right before I overheard you and Tate talking. It just seemed to confirm everything I thought about relationships and men. I couldn't risk going down that road again for something you thought was casual. I was already hurtling headfirst because I've been here before. With you."

He grasped her hand and squeezed. "Seven years ago."

"I know it wasn't more than a one-night stand for you, Erik. But for me, it was really special."

"Let me show you something." He released her hand and took out his phone. Scrolling through screens, he tapped and showed it to her. A text exchange.

"It's in Swedish."

"Oh, right." He did some more maneuvering on the screen. "Here, I've translated it. This is a conversation I had with my sister on Christmas Day after you fell asleep."

She began reading.

> ELSA
>
> I can't believe you told Casey about your condition.
>
> ERIK
>
> I want to be honest with her. It's important.
>
> ELSA
>
> Is it really her? That chick from before?
>
> ERIK
>
> Yes, it's a long story but I found her again.
>
> ELSA
>
> I can't wait to tell her what a baby you were about it back then. I can't find my Coco! Boo hoo, where's my sweet Coco?

> **ERIK**
> Shut up! Or I'll tell Dad that you broke the side mirror of the Volvo when you clipped the tree and that it wasn't some rando's fault like you claimed.

> **ELSA**
> That was twelve years ago!

> **ERIK**
> Like that'll help you.

> **ELSA**
> {Angry emoji} {Devil emoji} {Fox? Dog? emoji}

> **ELSA**
> Casey has no idea how evil you truly are. Evil and in love, the worst combination. I pity her.

> **ERIK**
> All I know is that I'll do whatever it takes to make this work.

That's where it cut off. Her heart thumped loudly, a rush of blood hitting her ears. He told his sister about his one-night stand. Who did that?

Erik "Fish" Jorgenson, that's who.

"Your sister knew about what happened between us seven years ago?"

"I used to call home a lot because I was so homesick and she and I have always been the closest. Though I don't know why because she has a twisted mind as you will learn when you get to know her better. I told her that I screwed up and couldn't find you. But I didn't want to come on too strong now because you would think I was strange. I'm trying not to be too pushy."

"I like pushy Erik. He knows what he wants."

"He is in love." His gaze was so clear and blue and true, as if he had never doubted anything or anyone. As if that was a completely normal thing to say.

And maybe it was. Maybe it was the *only* thing to say.

Damn.

She was in love with Erik Jorgenson. Had been for years. Yet, like any mere mortal with a keen sense of self-preservation, she had tried to relegate it to crush territory. It was the only way to get over him.

All this time, she'd been unable to put him out of her mind and heart. It was hard to forget the goalkeeper of your favorite hockey team, one of the assets you supported at your job, and the man who had taken your heart and mangled it. Twice.

But over the last week he had put it back together again, shard by shard, piece by piece.

Erik was here, telling her with words and actions that she was a big part of his life and that he wanted her to take center stage. If he could be honest, so could she.

"Erik, I've wanted you since the first second I laid eyes on you in the Empty Net. I fell for you and I don't think I ever quite got over you. Maybe it screwed up my relationship with Andrew—"

"Fuckface screwed up your relationship with Andrew."

Perhaps. But there may have always been some doubt about her commitment because her heart wasn't totally in the game. People could sense that. She sensed that with Andrew.

Both of them were going through the motions.

This didn't feel like that at all, but maybe it was the novelty. A new, exciting relationship with an NHL star. Only time would tell.

She wanted to take that time.

"What I'm trying to say is that I may not have been completely honest with him and I want to be with you. I want to get this right."

He placed his hands on her waist and pulled her close. "Is it so bad to get things wrong? Look at how we started, all the time we missed out on, all the moments lost. Some people might say that what has happened to us is some of the worst luck imaginable."

"Not just some people. I'd say that."

"Yet, I haven't given up. I refuse to." He held her gaze captive with a single-minded intensity that told her everything she needed. "I'm lonely. I don't mind admitting it. I have plenty of friends, the team, a job I love, but I want someone to spend my quiet moments with. Someone who needs me as much as I need her. Who turns me on, makes me laugh, and sees into the heart of me. I know you've been hurt, that you're feeling raw, that this might seem like a leap of faith because of what happened in the past between us. But since I figured out what I did wrong I think I've shown I can be trusted."

She could barely manage to choke out a response past the emotion clogging her throat. "You have. You absolutely have."

"Sometimes we'll get it right and sometimes we'll get it wrong. But we have to try. Would you like to try with me, Casey?"

Her heart was bursting, overflowing with love for this man.

"I'd love to."

He smiled and her world flooded with light. "Then we'll do exactly that."

And as he kissed her, she finally believed.

EPILOGUE

One year later ...

"God Jul!"

Everyone raised their glasses of glögg and toasted to the season before digging into the Jorgenson Julafton feast. Erik cast a glance around the table filled with his sisters and their husbands, his nieces and nephews (they seemed to multiply exponentially each year), and his parents looking on proudly. He caught his father's shining eyes and tried not to get too emotional himself. In their exchanged looks, a world of love was shared. After eight years, Erik had finally come home for Julafton.

He squeezed the thigh of the woman seated beside him. "Casey, you don't have to eat everything just to be polite."

She turned to him, her mouth full and gave him an eyebrow of "back off."

"Erik, let Coco eat all she wants," Elsa said. Everyone now knew the story of how he and Casey had met. The nickname had stuck, which Casey found to be hilarious.

"I just don't want her thinking she has to maintain eating pace with *you*, little monster."

Elsa scoffed. "Like anyone could." She put an entire slice of rye bread covered in pate in her mouth and swallowed it in one gulp.

"Sounds like a challenge," Casey said. "But I think I'll finish what's on my plate first." Admittedly it was piled high with something from every dish on the julbord. His woman was doing him proud.

Erik had made the trip back home this holiday because he had injured his wrist in November. It was almost back to 100%—though he'd had to endure the usual bawdy jokes from his teammates about *how* he had injured it—but he was given leave to take advantage of his time on IR and travel for a week to Örnsköldsvik. While Casey had spent plenty of time on his video calls with his family, he wanted to bring her home and introduce her properly.

Judging by the way she was putting her food away, she was fitting right in.

He ran a finger down her back and absorbed her shiver of pleasure. "Did you get a chance to talk to Kennedy?"

Casey nodded. "I did. Keanu is doing fine. Apparently he and Bucky are the best of friends, though from what I could see, it's pretty one-sided." Bucky was Reid Durand's dog.

"Keanu is being an asshole."

"You know it. Oh, it's risgrynsgröt, the Tomte porridge!" Casey's face lit up at the sight of the traditional pudding. Erik spooned some out for her into a small bowl and dusted it with cinnamon.

She tried it. "That's really good," then another bite, crunchier-sounding than the last, "I didn't expect nuts to be in it."

He caught his mother's knowing look and then his sister Astrid weighed in.

"If you get the almond, that means you have to"—she shot a sly glance Erik's way—"do the dishes."

His father spoke up. "She is a guest, she doesn't have to do anything."

"I don't mind doing dishes. I'm used to it because Erik does all the cooking."

Knowing how his mother and sisters would make trouble later, Erik figured he should get the jump on them. He leaned in and whispered to Casey, "There's another tradition tied to the person who finds the almond in the risgrynsgröt."

"You Swedes sure have a lot of traditions."

"We do. Whoever gets it will find true love in the coming year."

She licked her spoon in a way that made him hard in one place and soft in another. "What if she already has?"

"Then she will get married."

"Well, if it's tradition, no girl should try to fight that." Her eyes were bright with joy and laughter, and her smile would have knocked him over if he'd been standing.

"Thanks for coming home with me, Casey."

"Thanks for being my home." She kissed him, which produced a flurry of *aws* (adults except Elsa), *ews* (children plus Elsa), and a glow in his chest that assured him the rest of the trip would go well.

After the meal, he would take her for a walk around town and they would visit his old haunts. Maybe an amble down to the harbor to take in the lights across the bay or a tour of one of the many closets in his parents' home.

And then he would follow tradition and unveil the ring he had been carrying around for weeks. He hadn't had a lot of luck with stashing important things in pockets—that lost napkin had screwed him over—but he wasn't one for giving up. As the Swedes say, Ingen ko på isen, which translated to: *there's no cow on the ice.* It might have sounded like nonsense, but basically it was a recommendation to not worry. For the first time in forever, Erik was able to take that advice to heart.

Seven years of bad luck were over—he had found his Coco at last.

ACKNOWLEDGMENTS

Thanks to Kristi Yanta for overseeing another entry in the Rebels world, to Michele Catalano for a gorgeous Christmas-sexy cover (it's a word!), to Kim Cannon for another great copyedit, and to Julia Griffis for her fabulous attention to detail during the final proofread.

Erik is a Swede, a foodie, and a fan of all things Christmas, so I had to enlist the help of one of my Swedish readers to keep me on the straight and narrow. Linda Fredriksen was my go-to for Swedish Christmas traditions, food, and language, and I'm so grateful she took a few hours during her vacation to read Erik's story. Any mistakes that remain are all mine.

Finally, thanks to my loyal readers for your continued enjoyment of the Rebels. I couldn't do this without your encouragement and don't worry, there are more Rookie Rebels stories to be told. But for now, as Erik, would say "God Jul och Gott Nytt År." (That's Merry Christmas and Happy New Year.)

Until the next time,

Love, Kate

ABOUT THE AUTHOR

Originally from Ireland, *USA Today* bestselling author Kate Meader cut her romance reader teeth on Maeve Binchy and Jilly Cooper novels, with some Harlequins thrown in for variety. Give her tales about brooding mill owners, over-sexed equestrians, and men who can rock an apron, a fire hose, or a hockey stick, and she's there. Now based in Chicago, she writes sexy contemporary featuring strong heroes and amazing women and men who can match their guys quip for quip.

ALSO BY KATE MEADER

Rookie Rebels
GOOD GUY
INSTACRUSH
MAN DOWN
FOREPLAYER
DEAR ROOMIE
REBEL YULE
JOCK WANTED
SUPERSTAR
WILD RIDE

Chicago Rebels
IN SKATES TROUBLE
IRRESISTIBLE YOU
SO OVER YOU
UNDONE BY YOU
HOOKED ON YOU
WRAPPED UP IN YOU

Hot in Chicago Rookies
COMING IN HOT
UP IN SMOKE
DOWN IN FLAMES
HOT TO THE TOUCH

Laws of Attraction
DOWN WITH LOVE
ILLEGALLY YOURS
THEN CAME YOU

Hot in Chicago
REKINDLE THE FLAME
FLIRTING WITH FIRE
MELTING POINT
PLAYING WITH FIRE
SPARKING THE FIRE
FOREVER IN FIRE

Tall, Dark, and Texan
EVEN THE SCORE
TAKING THE SCORE
ONE WEEK TO SCORE

For updates, giveaways, and new release information, sign up for Kate's newsletter at katemeader.com.

Made in United States
North Haven, CT
28 June 2024